The Living

Schopenhauer

Bh. 200.

The Living Thoughts of
Schopenhauer

Thomas Mann

Rupa & Co

Copyright © Rupa & Co., 2002

Published 2002 by

Rupa . Co

7/16, Ansari Road, Daryaganj,
New Delhi 110 002

Sales Centres:

Allahabad Bangalore Chandigarh Chennai
Dehradun Hyderabad Jaipur Kathmandu
Kolkata Ludhiana Mumbai Pune

All rights reserved.
No part of this publication may be reproduced, stored in a
retrieval system, or transmitted, in any form or by any means,
electronic, mechanical, photocopying, recording or otherwise,
without the prior permission of the publishers.

ISBN 81-7167-976-5

By arrangement with original publishers

Typeset in 11 pts. Zapf Elliptical by
Nikita Overseas Pvt Ltd,
1410 Chiranjiv Tower,
43 Nehru Place
New Delhi 110 019

Printed in India by
Rekha Printers Pvt Ltd,
A-102/1 Okhla Industrial Area,
Phase-II, New Delhi-110 020

Contents

The Works of Arthur Schopenhauer

(1788-1860)

On the Fourfold Root of the Principle of Sufficient Reason
  (1813)
On Sight and Colours (1816)
The World as Will and Idea (1818)
On Will in Nature (1836)
On the Freedom of Man's Will
On the Basic Problems of Ethics (1841)
Parerga and Paralipomena (1851)

Schopenhauer

The pleasure we take in a metaphysical system, the gratification purveyed by the intellectual organization of the world into a closely reasoned, complete and balanced structure of thought, is always of a pre-eminently æsthetic kind. It flows from the same source as the satisfaction, the high and ever happy satisfaction we get from art, with its power to shape and order its material, to sort out life's manifold confusions so as to give us a clear and general view.

Truth and beauty must always be referred the one to the other. Each by itself, without the support given by the other, remains a very fluctuating value. Beauty which has not truth on its side and cannot have reference to it, does not live in it and through it, would be an empty chimæra— and "What is truth?" Our conceptions, created out of the phenomenal world, out of a highly conditioned point of view, are, as a critical and discriminating philosophy admits, applicable in an immanent, not in a transcendental sense—that is, they deal with knowledge vouchsafed to us in time, space and causality, and are conditioned by these, instead of being obtained by applying reason upon itself. The subject-matter of our thinking, and indeed the judgments we build up on it, are inadequate as a means of grasping the essence of things in themselves, the true essence of the world and of life. Even the most convinced and convincing, the most deeply experienced definition of that which underlies the manifestation, does not avail to get at the root of things and draw it to the light. What alone encourages the spirit of man in his persistent effort to do this is the necessary assumption that our own very being, the deepest thing in us, has the same universal basis, that it must of necessity root therein; and that accordingly we may be able to draw from it some data wherewith to clarify the relation of the world of phenomena with the true essence of things.

The history of Schopenhauerean thought goes back to the sources of the life of thought in our western world, whence issue European science and European art, and in which the two are still one. It goes back to Plato. The Greek philosopher taught that the things of this world have no real existence; they are always becoming, they never *are*. They are of no avail as objects of actual knowledge, for that can subsist only of what is in and of itself and always in the same way; whereas they, in their multiplicity and their purely relative, borrowed existence, which might as well be called non-existence, are never anything but the subject of an opinion based on sense-experience. They are shadows. The only things that have real existence, that always are and never pass away, are the actual originals of those shadows, the eternal ideas, the primeval forms of all things. These are not multiple, being by their very nature each unique, each the archetype, the shadows of imitations of which are merely like-named, ephemeral, individual things of the same kind. Ideas do not, like these, come up and die away; they are timeless and truly existent, not becoming and passing like their perishable imitations. Of them alone then can there be actual knowledge, as of that which always and in every respect *is*.

Obviously, it is the scientific spirit and training which teach us to subordinate to the idea the multiplicity of phenomena; which attribute truth and genuine reality to it alone and adhere to the contemplative abstraction and spiritualization of knowledge. Because of this discriminating distinction between the phenomenon and the idea, between the empiric and the intellectual, between the world of truth and the world of appearance, between the temporal and the eternal, the life of Plato was a very great event in the history of the human spirit; and first of all it was a scientific and a moral event. Everyone feels that something profoundly moral attaches to this elevation of the ideal as the only actual, above the ephemeralness and multiplicity of the phenomenal, this devaluation of the senses to the advantage of the spirit, of the temporal to the advantage of the eternal—quite in the spirit of the Christianity which came after it. For in a way the transitory phenomenon, and the sensual attaching to it, are put thereby into a state of sin: he alone finds truth and salvation who turns his face to the eternal. From this point of view Plato's philosophy exhibits the connection between science and ascetic morality.

But it exhibits another relationship: that with the world of art. According to such a philosophy time itself is merely the partial and piecemeal view which an individual holds of ideas—the latter, being outside time, are thus eternal. "Time"—so runs a beautiful phrase of Plato— "is the moving image of eternity." And so this pre-Christian, already Christian doctrine, with all its ascetic wisdom, possesses on the other hand extraordinary charm of a sensuous and creative kind: for a conception of the world as a colourful and moving phantasmagoria of pictures, which are transparencies for the ideal and the spiritual, eminently savours of the world of art, and through it the artist first comes into this own. He it is who may owe his bond to the world of images and appearances—be sensually, voluptuously, sinfully bound to them, yet be aware at the same time that he belongs no less to the world of the idea and the spirit, as the magician who makes the appearance transparent that the idea and spirit may shine through. Here is exhibited the artist's mediating task, his hermetic and magical rôle as broker between the upper and the lower world, between idea and phenomenon, spirit and sense. Here, in fact, we have what I may call the cosmic position of art; her unique mission in he world, the high dignity—which flings dignity away— of her functioning, can be defined or explained in no other way.

Plato as artist. I hold that a philosophy is valid not only—sometimes least of all—by reason of its ethical teaching, by the doctrine which it links to its interpretation of the world and its experience of it; but also and especially through this very experience itself. This indeed—not the spiritual and ethical concomitant of its doctrine of truth and salvation—is the essential, primary and personal part of a philosophy. If one divorce from a philosopher his philosophy there is much left; and it would be a pity if there were not. Nietzsche, the intellectually apostate pupil of Schopenhauer, wrote of his master:

> "What he *taught* is put aside;
> What he *lived*, that will abide—
> Behold a man!
> Subject he was to none."

The philosophy of Schopenhauer which I am about to discuss, its validity and dynamic power, proved as liable to abuse as the ascetic, scientific and creatively fruitful message of Plato. I refer here to the exploitation which Schopenhauer suffered at the hands of a colossally gifted artist, Richard Wagner—of this perhaps more at another time. But whosesoever the blame, it certainly does not lie at the door of Schopenhauer's other teacher and inspirer, who contributed to the structure of his system. I mean, of course Kant. Kant's bent was exclusively and positively on the side of mind—very much aloof from art but by so much the closer to critique.

Immanuel Kant, the critic of pure knowledge, rescued philosophy from the speculation into which it had retreated and brought it back into the realm of the human intellect; made this his field and delimited the reason. At

Königsberg in Prussia, in the second half of the eighteenth century, he was teaching something very like the premises laid down two thousand years before by the Athenian thinker. Our whole experience of the world, he declared, is subject to three laws and conditions, the inviolable forms in which all our knowledge is effectuated. These are time, space and causality. But they are not definitions of the world as it may be in and for itself, of *Das Ding an sich*, independently of our apperception of it; rather they belong only to its appearance, in that they are nothing but the forms of our knowledge. All variation, all becoming and passing away is only possible through these three. Thus they depend only on appearance and we can know nothing through them of the "thing in itself" to which they are in no way applicable. This fact applies even to our own ego: we apprehend it only as manifestation, not as anything which it may be in itself. In other words, time, space and causality are mechanisms of the intellect, and as I have said above, we call immanent the conception of things which is vouchsafed to us in their image and conditioned by them; while that is transcendent which we might gain by applying reason upon itself, by critique of the reason, and by dint of seeing through these three devices as mere forms of knowledge.

This is Kant's fundamental concept; and as we can see, it is closely related to Plato's. Both explain the visible world as phenomenal, in other words as idle seeming, which gains significance and some measure of reality only by virtue of that which shines through it. For both Plato and Kant, the true reality lies above, behind, in short "beyond" the phenomenon. Whether it was called "idea" or *"Das Ding an sich"* is relatively unimportant.

Both these concepts penetrated deeply into Schopenhauer's thought. He early elected the exhaustive study of Plato and Kant (Göttingen, 1809-11) and placed above all others these two philosophers so widely separated in time and space. He took from them what he could use, and it gratified his craving for the traditional that he could so well use it; although due to his entirely different constitution—so much more "modern," storm-tossed and suffering—he made out of it something else altogether.

What he took was the "idea" and the *"Ding an sich."* But with the latter he did something very bold, even scarcely permissible, though at the same time with deeply felt, almost compulsive conviction: he defined the *Ding an sich,* he called it by name, he asserted—though from Kant himself you would never have known—that he knew what it was. It was the Will. The will was the ultimate, irreducible, primeval principle of being, the source of all phenomena, the begetter present and active in every single one of them, the impelling force producing the whole visible world and all life—for it was the will to live. It was this through and through; so that whoever said "will" was speaking of the will to live, and if you used the longer term you were guilty of a pleonasm. The will always willed one thing: life. And why? Because it found it priceless? Because it afforded the experience of any objective knowledge of life? Ah, no. All knowledge alike was foreign to the will; it was something independent of knowledge, it was entirely original and absolute, a blind urge, a fundamental, uncausated, utterly unmotivated impulse; so far from depending on any evaluation of life, the converse was the case, and all judgments were dependent upon the strength of the will to live.

The will, then, this "in-itself-ness" of things, existing outside time, space and causality blind and causeless, greedily, wildly, ruthlessly demanded life, demanded *objectivation;* and this objectivation occurred in such a way that its original unity became a multiplicity—a process which received the appropriate name of the *principium individuationis* (the principle of individuality). The will, avid of life, to wreak its desire objectivated itself in accordance with the *principium*, thus dispersing itself into the myriad parts of the phenomenal world existing in time and space; but at the same time it remained in full strength in each single and smallest of those parts. The world, then, was the product and the expression of the will, the objectivation of the will in space and time. But it was at the same time something else besides: it was the *idea*, my idea and yours, the idea of each one and each one's idea about himself—by virtue, that is, of the discerning mind, which the will created to be a light to it in the higher stages of its objectivation. Note that it was not the intellect which brought forth the will; the converse was the case, the will brought forth the intellect. It was not intellect, mind, knowledge that was the primary and dominant factor; it was the will, and the intellect served it. And how could it have been otherwise, since after all enough knowledge even for the objectivation of will belonged to a later stage and without will simply had no chance to appear? In a world entirely the work of will, of absolute, unmotivated, causeless and unvaluated life-urge, intellect had of course only second place. Sensibility, nerves, brain, were—just like the other parts of the organism and quite specifically like the sex organs, the opposite pole of the discerning brain—an expression of the will at a given phase of its objectivation. And the idea, coming into being through the will, was just as much intended to serve it and just as little an end in itself, as were those other parts. This relation between will and mind, this premise of Schopenhauer that the second is only the tool of the first, has about it much that is humiliating and deplorable, much that is even comic. It puts in a nutshell the whole tendency and capacity of mankind to delude itself and imagine that its will receives its direction and content from its mind, whereas our philosopher asserts the direct opposite, and relegates the intellect—apart from its duty of shedding a little light on the immediate surroundings of the will and aiding it to achieve the higher states of its struggle for life—to a position as mere mouthpiece of the will: to justify it, to provide it with "moral" motivations and in short to rationalize our instincts.

It was a remarkably pessimistic valuation. Indeed, all the text-books tell us that Schopenhauer is first the philosopher of the will and second the philosopher of pessimism. But actually there is no first and second, for they are one and the same, and he was the second because and by virtue of his being the first; he was necessarily pessimist because he was the philosopher and psychologist of the will. Will, as the opposite pole of inactive satisfaction, is naturally a fundamental unhappiness, it is unrest, a striving for *something*—it is want, craving, acidity, demand, suffering; and a world of will can be nothing else but a world of suffering. The will, objectivating itself in all existing things, quite literally wreaks on the physical its metaphysical craving; satisfies that craving in the most frightful way in the world and through the world which it has brought forth, and which, born of greed and compulsion, turns out to be a thing to shudder at. In other words, will becoming world according to the *principium individuationis,* and being dispersed into a multiplicity of parts, forgets its original unity and, although in all its divisions it remains essentially one, it becomes will a million times divided against itself. Thus it strives against itself, seeking its own well-being in each of the millions of its manifestations, its place in the sun at the expense of another, yes, at the expense of all others, and so constantly sets its teeth in its own flesh, like that dweller in Tartarus who avidly devoured his own members. This is meant in a literal sense. Plato's "ideas" have in Schopenhauer become incurably gluttonous. As various stages of the objectivation of the will, space, time and matter fall upon each other. The plant world has to serve as nourishment for the animal, each animal for another as prey and food, and thus the will to live gnaws for ever at itself. And lastly man sees the whole created for his use but in his turn makes frightfully explicit the horror of the struggle of all against all, the division of the will against itself. We express all this in the phrase *homo homini lupus*.

Everywhere that Schopenhauer takes occasion to talk of the anguish of the world and the rage for life of the will's multiple incarnations (and he talks much and explicitly about them) his extraordinary native eloquence, his genius as a writer, reach their utmost height of icy brilliance. He speaks with a cutting vehemence, in accents of experience and all-embracing knowledge that horrify and bewitch us by their power and veracity. Certain pages display a fierce and caustic mockery of life, uttered as it were with flashing eyes and compressed lips, and in a shower of Greek and Latin quotations: a pitiful-pitiless coruscation of statement, citation and proof of the utter misery of the world. All this is far from being so depressing as one would expect from the pitch of acuity and sinister eloquence it arrives at. Actually it fills the reader with strange, deep satisfaction, whose source is the spiritual rebellion speaking in the words, the human indignation betrayed in what seems like a suppressed quiver of the voice. Everyone feels this satisfaction; everyone realizes that when this great writer and commanding spirit speaks of the suffering of the world, he speaks of yours and mine; all of us feel what amounts almost to triumph at being thus avenged by the heroic word.

Poverty, need, concern for the mere preservation of life—these come first. Then when they are painfully allayed, come sexual urge, the sufferings of love, jealousy, envy, hatred, fear, ambition, avarice, illness—and so on and so on, without end. All the evils whose source is the inner conflict of the will come out of Pandora's box. And what is left at the bottom? Hope? Ah, no. Satiety, tedium. For between pain and satiety every human being is tossed to and fro. The pain is positive, the pleasure merely the absence of pain—a negative, passing over at once into boredom, just as the tonic to which the melodic labyrinth leads back, just as the harmony in which disharmony issues, would bore us intolerably if they went on and on. Are there real satisfactions? They exits. But compared with the long torture of our desires, the endlessness of our requirements, they are short and scant, and to one gratified desire there are at least ten which remain unstilled. Moreover the appeasement itself is only apparent, for the fulfilled desire soon makes a new vacancy—the first is now a known error, the second still unknown. No achieved object of desire can give lasting satisfaction. It is like alms thrown to a beggar, which merely linger out from day to day his miserable life. Happiness? It would be in repose. But precisely this is impossible for him who feels desire. To flee, to pursue, to fear disaster, to covet pleasure—it is all one: preoccupation with the will's incessant demands fills and animates the consciousness without cease, and thus the subject of the willing lies ever on Ixion's turning wheel, takes up water in the sieve of the Danaides and plays the ever-toiling Tantalus.

But yet: there *is* release from miseries and mistakes, from the errors and penalties of this life. This gift is laid in the hand of the human being, the highest and most developed objectivation of the will and accordingly the most richly capable of suffering. Would you think the gift might be death? Not at all. Death belongs utterly and entirely to the sphere of the phenomenal, the empirical, the sphere of change. It has no contact with transcendent and true actuality. What is mortal in us is merely the individuation; the core of our being, the will, which is the will to live, remains entirely unassailed, and can, if it continue to affirm itself, find out fresh avenues of approach to life. Herein, may I say in passing, resides the folly and immorality of suicide: in its futility. For the individual denies and destroys only his individuation, not the original error, the will to live, which in suicide is only seeking a route to more complete realization. So, then, not death. Redemption bears quite another name and has quite a different conditioning. One does not suspect the mediator to be thanked for this blessing when it comes. It is the intellect.

But the intellect—is it not the creature of the will, its instrument, its light in the darkness, destined only for its service? It is, and so remains. And yet—not always, not in all cases. Under peculiar, happy—ah, verily, under blissful—conditions; in exceptional circumstances, then, the servant and poor tool may become the master of his master and creator, may get the better of him, emancipate himself, achieve his own independence, and, at least at times, assert his single sovereignty, his mild, serene and all-embracing rule. Then the will, put aside and shorn of power, falls into a bland and peaceful decline. There is a state, where the miracle comes to pass, that knowledge wrenches itself free from will, the subject ceases to be merely individual and becomes the pure, will-less subject of knowledge. We may call it the æsthetic state. This is one of the greatest and profoundest of Schopenhauer's perceptions. And however frightful the accents he commands in describing the tortures of the will and the domination of the will, in equal degree his prose discovers seraphic tones, his gratitude speaks with surpassing exuberance, when abundantly and exhaustively he discourses of the blessings of art. The intellectual formulation and interpretation of this, perhaps Schopenhauer's most personal experience, he owes to his teachers, Plato and Kant. "Beautiful," Kant had declared, "is what happens without *interest.*" Without interest. That, for Schopenhauer, and rightly, meant without reference to the will. The æsthetic gratification was pure, disinterested, free from will; it was clear, unclouded, profoundly satisfied contemplation. And why was it that? Here Plato came in, with the latent æstheticism of his philosophy of ideas. Ideas. They it was, for which, in the æsthetic state, phenomena, the mere images of eternity, became transparent. The eyes opened upon ideas—and here was the great, pure, sunny, objective contemplation, by which alone the genius—and even he only in his creative hours and moments—and with him his audience, was justified of his æsthetic achievement.

Apollo, god of the muses, "he who shoots his arrows from afar," is a god of distance, of space, not of pathos and pathology or involvement with the painful. He is an objective god the god of irony. In irony, then, as Schopenhauer saw it, in creative objectivity, knowledge was freed from its bondage to will, and the attention was no longer blurred by any purpose. We reached a state of selfless resignation, where reference was had to things as sheer ideas, no longer as purposes; and a peace heretofore unknown was all at once vouchsafed us. "It is," says our author, "wholly well with us. It is the painless state praised by Epicurus as the highest good and the state of the gods; we are, for that moment, released from the base urge of the will, we celebrate the sabbath of our toil in the prison-house of will, the wheel of Ixion stands still."

Famous, oft-quoted words, lured from this bitter and tormented soul by the vision of the beautiful and the peace it purveyed. Are they true? But what is truth? An experience that finds such words to describe itself must be true, must be justified by the power of its feeling. Or should we believe that these words of sheer and boundless gratitude were coined to describe a relative, at bottom a merely negative, happiness? For happiness anyhow is negative, it is the surcease of torment; and even in all our glad objective contemplation of æsthetic ideas it cannot be other than the same. Schopenhauer, in the choice of the images he is inspired to use, unequivocally reveals the fact. This happiness too is temporal, transitory. The creative state, so he found, the sojourn among images irradiated by the idea—these would not bring the final redemption. The æsthetic state was but the prior stage to a perfected one, in which the will, not permanently satisfied in the æsthetic, would be once for all outshone by knowledge, would void the field and be annihilated. The consummation of the artist would be the saint.

What, after all, is ethic? It is the philosophy of the

actions of human beings, the teaching of good and evil. The teaching? Then was the will, blind, causeless and senseless as it was, teachable? Certainly not. Certainly virtue was not a thing to be learned; no more than was art. Just as a man could not become an artist by having explained to him the essence of the creative state, so he could not shun evil and ensue good by instruction in the nature of the one and the other. No prescriptions could be issued to the will. It was free, absolute, all-powerful. Freedom, indeed, dwelt in the will alone, thus it existed wholly in transcendence, never in the empiric world, which was the objectivation of the world subsisting in time, space and causality. Here everything was strictly casual, bound and determined by cause and effect. Freedom, like the will, was beyond and on the other side of the phenomenal, but there it was present and dominant, and therein lay the freedom of the will. As so often, the situation respecting freedom was just contrary to that conceived by ordinary common sense. It lay not in doing but in being, not in *operari* but in *esse*. In *doing*, indeed, then, inevitable necessity and determinacy reigned; while *being* was originally and metaphysically free. The human being who performed a culpable action had indeed so *acted* of necessity, as a being existing in the realm of the empiric, and under the influence of definite motives. But he could have *been* different; and his fear, his pangs of conscience, also had reference to his being, not his doing.

A harsh, cruel thought—arrogant, offensive, ruthless. To accept it runs contrary to our feelings—and yet it is precisely our feelings which are challenged by its mysticism. For it has at the bottom of it a mystic truth, by virtue of which the twin conceptions of merit and demerit, far from being invalidated, become even more profound and awe-inspiring. They are, of course, divorced thereby from the moral sphere as such. But aristocratic intellects, not much concerned with considerations of "justice," have always been inclined to favour this divorce. Goethe liked to talk of "inborn merits," an absurd phrase from any logical or ethical point of view. For "merit" is entirely and by definition an ethical concept; whereas what is inborn—be it beauty, talent, wit, refinement, or, in the sphere of outward destiny, good fortune—can thus not logically be merits. In order to speak of merit in this sense it must be the issue of choice, the expression of a will antecedent to the phenomenon. And this is just what Schopenhauer asserts when he harshly and haughtily declares that each of us, blest or unblest, gets exactly what he deserves.

But this aristocratic complaisance at injustice and the varied lot of mortals is soon enough resolved in the most peremptory and democratic equality; simply because the variations—and even the differentiation itself—are shown to be an illusion. Schopenhauer calls this illusion by a name drawn from Hindu metaphysics, which he greatly admires because of its pessimistic harmony with his own account of the world: he calls it the "veil of Maya." But much earlier he had, as occidental scholars do, clothed it in Latin, thus: he says that the great illusion of inequality and injustice in the character, situation and fate of individuals rest on the *principium individuationis.* Variation, inequality, are only attributes of multiplicity in time and space. That is to say, they are mere appearance, the notion which we, as individuals, thanks to the organization of the intellect, have of a world which in reality is the objectivation of the will to live, in the general and in the particular, in you and in me. But the individual, with his strong sense of being separate and set apart form the universe, does not recognize this—how could he, when the conditioning of his knowledge, the "veil of Maya," enfolding his vision and the outlying world, prevents him from getting sight of the truth? The individual does not see the essence of things, which is one, but its manifestations, which he beholds as separate and differing, yes, even opposed: pleasure and pain, the tormentor and the tormented, the joyous life of one and the other's wretched lot. You affirm, that is, for yourself, the one, and deny, with special reference to yourself, the other. The will, which is your origin and essence, makes you demand good fortune and the enjoyment of existence. You stretch out your hands for them, you press them to you, and it escapes your notice that when you thus affirm these as goods you affirm at the same time all the evils, all the torments in the world and press them no less to your heart. The evil that you do thereby, the evil that you inflict; on the other hand your indignation at the world's injustice, your envy, yearning and desire, your cosmic craving—all these come from the delusion of multiplicity, the false belief that you are not the world and the world is not you. All this comes from the illusion of Maya, from the illusory distinction between the I and the you.

Thence, likewise, comes your fear of death. Death is

only the setting right of an error, a confusion—for every individual is a confusion. Death is nothing but the disappearance of an imaginary partition-wall shutting off the I you are enclosed in from the rest of the world. You believe that when you die this rest of the word will go on existing, while you, horrible to say, will be no more. But I say to you, this world, which is your idea, will no longer be; whereas you, precisely that in you which, because it is the will to live, fears death and rejects it, *you* will remain, will live. For the will, out of which you have your being, will always know how to find the gate of life. To it all eternity belongs; and together with life, which it recognizes as time, though actually it is perpetual present, time too will be vouchsafed you again. Your will, so long as it wills, is always sure of life, with all its torments and blisses. Better it were for you if it were not.

Meanwhile you live, as he who you are. You see and love, you look and long, you covet the unknown image of your desire—ah, so strange and different from yourself!—you suffer for it, you long to draw it to your heart, to draw it into you, to *be* it. But to be a thing is something quite different, and incomparably more grievous and onerous than to see it. The longing set up by the idea is all a delusion. You yourself are given to yourself, your body is given to you, as idea, as all the rest of the world is. But at the same time it is given to you as will—the only thing in the world which is given you at the same time as will. Everything else is for you only idea. The universe is, so to speak, a play, ballet; all your natural, instinctive convictions tell you that it has nothing like the same reality as you, the spectator, have; that it is not to be taken with anything like the same seriousness as you yourself are. Trapped in the *principium individuationis,* shrouded in the veil of Maya, the ego sees all other forms of life as masks and phantoms, and is simply incapable of ascribing anything like the same importance or seriousness to them as to itself. Are not you the only actually existent thing, are you not all that matters? You are the navel of the world; if it be well with you, if the afflictions of this life be kept as far from you as possible, its blisses as near, that is the one vital thing. What happens to others is nothing by comparison. It does you neither good nor harm.

Such is the conviction of native, unbroken and quite unenlightened egotism; absolute prepossession with the *principium individuationis*. To see through this principle, to divine its illusory, truth-shrouding character; to begin to perceive that the I and the you are indistinguishable the one from the other; to have the emotional intuition that the will is the same in the one and the all: such is the beginning and the essence of ethics. Evil is that man who, so soon as no other outer power prevents him, inflicts evil. I mean a man who, not content with affirming the will to live as manifested in his own body, also denies the will manifest in other individuals and seeks to destroy their existence as soon as it is in the way of his own efforts. A wild, untamed will, one not content with the affirmation of his own body, speaks in the bad character. But there is above all so profound a prejudice in favour of the manifestation and the *principium individuationis* that it clings with iron grip to the distinctions fixed by the *principium* between its own person and all others. And accordingly it considers the existence of others wholly foreign to its own, severed from it by a deep abyss. It regards them as empty shells, and cherishes a profound conviction that reality is an attribute of itself alone.

Goodness is positive. It performs the service of love. Its motive is profoundly emotional: were it not to do so, it would seem to itself like a man who starves today in order tomorrow to have more than he can eat. Just so it would seem to the good man, to let others famish while he lived in abundance. For such a one the veil of Maya has become transparent, he has lost the great illusion whereby will, in its multiple manifestations, here starves and suffers, there enjoys, because it is after all the same will, and the same torture, which he thus both invokes and suffers. Love and goodness are *sympathy*—in recognition of the "*Tat twam asi*," the "this thou art," when the veil of Maya is lifted. Spinoza said: "*Benevolentia nihil aliud est, quam cupidatas ex commiseratione orta*" (Goodness is nothing else than love born of sympathy). But from this it is clear that as justice can rise to heights of goodness, so goodness in its turn can rise to greater heights: not only to most disinterested love and most magnanimous self-sacrifice, but verily to saintliness. For a man with such knowledge of love will regard the suffering of everything living as his own suffering, and make his own the pain of all the world. He sees the whole: sees life as an internal conflict; and continual pain, suffering humanity, suffering animal world and the knowledge of the essence of things in themselves combine to lay a quieting hand upon his will. In him will turns away from life. Obliged, in his sympathetic understanding, to deny life, how then can he affirm even in himself the will to live, life being but the work, mirror and expression of will? Thus to recognize, thus to resolve, means renunciation, means the ultimate quietism. And so it comes about that virtue passes over into *ascesis;* and this is a paradox, truly a high and great one: an individuation of the will here rejects the essence manifesting and expressing itself in its very own body. Its acts give the lie to its manifestation, they openly controvert it. The ascetic rejects the satisfactions of sex. His chastity is the sign that with the life of the body likewise the life of the will abrogates itself. What is the mark of the saint? That he does nothing of all that he would like to do, and does all that he does not like to do. If ascetic chastity were to become a general practice, it would bring about the end of the human race. And since all manifestations of the will are one, with man, the highest of these, would also fall away his feebler copy, the animal kingdom. All knowledge would fail, and since without subject there is no object all the rest of the visible world would dissolve and melt away. Man is the potential redeemer of nature. The mystic Angelus Silesius says:

> "O man, all living love thee; they press about thee,
> They run to thee that they may reach their god."

Schopenhauer—all his misanthropy notwithstanding and all that he says about the corrupt condition of life in general and the distortions of the spirit of man in particular; notwithstanding his despair over the wretched

social state one is born into as a human being—
Schopenhauer is humanly full of pride and reverence as
he contemplates the "crown of creation." To him the words
mean, just as they did to the author of Genesis, man, the
highest and most developed objectivation of the will. This
most significant form of Schopenhauer's humanism
perfectly—if by implication—accords with his political
scepticism, his anti-revolutionarism. Man, according to
him, is to be reverenced because he is the *knowing*
creature. All knowing, of course, is fundamentally subject
to the will out of which it sprang just as the head springs
from the trunk. In the animal kingdom, indeed, this
subjection of the intellect is never overcome. But look at
the difference between man and beast in this relation
between head and trunk. In the lower animal kingdom
they are completely grown together, and in all animals the
head is inclined to the earth, where lie the objects of the
will; yes, even in the higher animals head and trunk are
much more one than in man, whose head (Schopenhauer
here uses the German word *Haupt*, to make the distinction
clear) appears to be independently set on the shoulders,
and uses the body to carry it, instead of being subject to
it. This human advantage is shown pre-eminently in the
Apollo Belvedere. The god of the muses carries his mobile,
wide-eyed head so easily on his shoulders that it seems
to have escaped from the body and there is no need to take
further interest in it.

What association of ideas could be more humanistic
than this? Not for nothing does Schopenhauer choose the
statue of the god of the muses as the image of human

dignity. Art, knowledge and the dignity of human suffering are here envisaged as one—a profound and significant perception of our pessimistic humanist. And since humanism in general is prone to rhetoric and the wearing of rose-tinted spectacles, we have here something quite new, and, I venture to assert, something in the realm of ideas considerably in advance of its time. In the human being, the highest objectivation of the will, the latter is most brightly irradiated by knowledge. But in equal measure as knowledge arrives at clarity, the consciousness is heightened, the suffering increases, and thus in man it reaches its highest point. Even in individuals it varies in degree. "The degree of suffering," says Nietzsche, "is determined by the position in the hierarchy." Here Nietzsche betrays his ultimate dependence upon Schopenhauer's aristocratic theory of man's noble vocation to suffer. And in particular the highest type of man, the genius. It is this vocation that gives rise to the two great possibilities which Schopenhauer's humanism envisages for man. They are: art and consecration. Only the human being possesses the possibility of the æsthetic state, as "disinterested" contemplation of the idea; to humanity alone is it given to achieve the final redemption, the renunciation of the will to live, as the artist mounts to the still loftier stage of ascetic saintliness. To man is vouchsafed the opportunity to right the wrong, to reverse the great error and mistake of being; to get the supreme insight which teaches him to make the suffering of the whole world his own and can lead him to renunciation and the conversion of the will. And so man is the secret hope of the world and of all creatures; towards whom as it were all creation trustfully turns as to its hoped-for redeemer and saviour.

This is a conception of great mystical beauty. It expresses a humane reverence for the mission of man, such as outweighs all misanthropy and supplies the corrective to all Schopenhauer's loathing of humanity. To me the importance of it lies in this union of pessimism and humanism, revealed to us by the philosopher: the assertion that the one in no wise excludes the other, and that in order to be a humanist one does not need to be a rhetorical flatterer of humanity.

But we should be careful not to take too literally or seriously Schopenhauer's humanistic attitude or his classical, Apollonian pronouncements. In his case, as in many others, we must distinguish between the person and the opinion, the human being and his judgments. What warns us is Schopenhauer's extremist position, a grotesque and dualistic antithesis in his nature, a romanticism (in the most colourful sense of the word) which removed him further from the Goethean sphere than he would ever have let himself even dream of.

Seldom has a book had a more expressive, more exhaustive title than Schopenhauer's chief work, his only work, in truth, developing his own original train of thought. All else that he wrote in a lifetime of seventy-two years only forms an assiduously collected accompaniment and reinforcement to it. *The World as Will and Idea*. That is not only the theme, in its most compendious formulation: it is the man, the human being, his personality, his life, his suffering. The compulsive force of this man, and in particular his sexual urge, must have been enormous—cruel and tortuous as are the mythological figures he employs to describe the bondage to the will. It must have opposed with such equal power the compulsive force of his urge for knowledge, his lucid and mighty intellectuality, as to produce a frightfully radical duality and conflict, with a correspondingly profound craving for release; and to issue in the intellectual denial of life itself, the impeachment of his own essence as evil, erroneous and culpable. Rightly, if in an elevated sense, one may call this tortuous and grotesque. Sex is to Schopenhauer the focal point of the will; in its physical objectivation the opposite pole of the brain, which represented knowledge. Obviously, his capacity in both spheres went far beyond the average; though that in itself would only speak for the intensity and range of his nature. What makes him a pessimist, a *denier* of the world, is just the contradictory and hostile, exclusive and anguishing relation of the two spheres to each other. We need not, though it would be easy to do so, fail to understand his pessimism as the intellectual product of that very richness and power. Here is a bi-polar nature, full of contrasts and conflicts, tortured and violent; after its own pattern it must experience the world: as instinct and spirit, passion and knowledge, "will" and "idea." But suppose he had learned to reconcile them in his genius, in his creative life. Suppose he had understood that genius does not at all consist in sensuality put out of action and will unhinged, that art is not mere objectivation of spirit, but the fruitful union and interpenetration of both spheres, immensely heightening to life and more fascinating than either can be by itself! That the essence of the creative artist is nothing else—and in Schopenhauer himself was nothing else—than sensuality spiritualized, than spirit informed and made creative by sex! Goethe's interpretation and experience differed from the pessimist's; it was happier, healthier, more blithely "classic," less pathologic (I use the word in its rarer, unclinical sense)—less romantic, shall I say? For Goethe, sex and spirit (mind) were the highest, most provocative charms in life. He wrote: *"Denn das Leben ist die Liebe, und des Lebens Leben—Geist"* (For life is love, and spirit the life of life). But in Schopenhauer genius intensified both spheres until they took refuge in the ascetic. To him, sex is of the devil, a diabolic distraction from pure contemplation; knowledge is that denial of sex which says: "If thine eye offend thee, pluck it out." Knowledge as "peace of the soul," art as a sedative and liberating condition of pure contemplation unmarred by will; the artist as a half-way stage to sainthood, divorced from the will to live: that is Schopenhauer. And again, in so far as this conception of mind and art is objective, it approaches Goethe's, it has a classic cast. But being exaggerated and ascetic, it is definitely romantic, in one sense of the word, and that would not have appealed to Goethe—as witness his attitude of Heinrich von Kleist.

But after all, terms and antitheses like classic and romantic do not apply to Schopenhauer. Neither the one nor the other is adequate to describe a mentality later in time than those for whom they once played their rôle. He stands nearer to us than do the minds who in their day were occupied with such distinctions and ranged themselves accordingly. Schopenhauer's mental life, the dualistic, overstrained irritability and fever of his genius is less romantic than it is modern. I should like to enlarge upon this distinction, but content myself with making it refer in general to a state of mind the increasing strain of which became only too marked in our western world in the century between Goethe and Nietzsche. In this respect Schopenhauer stands between the two, he makes a bridge between them: more "modern," more suffering and difficult than Goethe, but much more "classic," robust and healthy than Nietzsche. From which it is clear that optimism and pessimism, the affirmation or denial of life, have nothing to do with health and illness. Illness and health, accordingly, have to be used with great caution as criteria or valuations. They are biological conceptions, whereas the nature of man is not exhausted in the biological.

Schopenhauer, as psychologist of the will, is the father of all modern psychology. From him the line runs, by way of the psychological radicalism of Nietzsche, straight to Freud and the men who built up his psychology of the unconscious and applied it to the mental sciences. Nietzsche's anti-socratism and hostility to mind are nothing but the philosophic affirmation and glorification of Schopenhauer's discovery of the primacy of the will, his pessimistic insight into the secondary and subservient relation of mind to will. He makes the statement, certainly not humane in the classical sense, that the intellect is there to do the pleasure of the will, to justify it, to provide it with motivations which are often very shallow and self-deluding, in fine to rationalize the instincts. It is a sceptical and pessimistic psychology, an analysis of relentless penetration. And it not only prepared the way for what we call psychoanalysis, it was already just that. At bottom all psychology is the unmasking, the acute, ironic, naturalistic perception of the riddling relation that obtains between the reason and the instincts. A little dialogue in the *Wahlverwandtschaften* well illustrates this underhand game our natures play. Eduard, already in love after his first meeting with Ottilie, is made by Goethe to say: "She is a highly intelligent person." To which his wife replies: "Intelligent? She never opened her mouth." Schopenhauer must certainly have enjoyed this passage. It is a pleasant, blithely classic illustration of his own thesis, that one does not want a thing because it is good, but finds it good because one wants it.

This essay is an attempt to evoke to-day a figure little known to the present generation; and to reconsider and recapitulate his concepts. Its object is to reassert the idea of the connection between pessimism and humanism. I should like to hand on, to a world where human feeling is today finding itself in sore straits, the knowledge of this combined melancholy and pride in the human race which make up Schopenhauer's philosophy. His pessimism—that is his humanity. His interpretation of the world by the concept of the will, his insight into the overweening power of instinct and the derogation of the one-time god-like reason, mind and intellect to a mere tool with which to achieve security—all this is anti-classic and in its essence inhumane. But it is precisely in the pessimistic hue of his philosophy that his humanity and spirituality lie; in the fact that this great artist, practised in suffering and wielding the pros of a great humane cultural epoch in our history, lifts man out of the biological sphere of nature, makes his own feeling and understanding soul the theatre where the will meets its reverse, and sees in the human being the saviour of all creation.

The twentieth century has in its first third taken up a position of reaction against classic rationalism and intellectualism. It has surrendered to admiration of the unconscious, to a glorification of instinct, which it thinks is overdue to life. And the bad instincts have accordingly been enjoying a heyday. We have seen instead of pessimistic conviction deliberate malice. Intellectual recognition of bitter truth turns into hatred and contempt for mind itself. Man has greedily flung himself on the side of "life"—that is, on the side of the stronger—for there is no disputing the fact that life has nothing to fear from mind, that not life but knowledge, or rather, mind, is the weaker part and one more needing protection on this earth. Yet the anti-humanity of our day is a humane experiment too in its way. It is a one-sided answer to the eternal question as to the nature and destiny of man. We palpably need a corrective to restore the balance, and I think the philosophy I here evoke can do good service. I spoke of Schopenhauer as modern. I might have called him futurist. The chiaroscuro harmonies of his human traits, the mixture in him of Voltaire and Jacob Böhme;[1]

1. Jacob Böhme, German mystic, 1575-1924.

the paradox of his classic, pellucid prose, employed to lighten the darkest and lowest purlieus of being; his proud misanthropy, which never belies his reverence for the idea of the human being; in short, what I called his pessimistic humanity, seems to me to herald the temper of a future time. Once he was fashionable and famous, then half-forgotten. But his philosophy may still exert a ripe and humanizing influence upon our age. His intellectual sensitivity, his teaching, which was life, that knowledge, thought and philosophy are not matters of the head alone but of the whole man, heart and sense, body and soul; in other words, his existence as an artist may help to bring to birth a new humanity to which we stand in need, and to which they are akin: a humanity above dry reason on the one hand and idolatry of instinct on the other. For art, accompanying man on his painful journey to self-realization, has always been before him at the goal.

First Book
The World as Idea

First Aspect

THE IDEA SUBORDINATED TO THE PRINCIPLE OF SUFFICIENT
REASON: THE OBJECT OF EXPERIENCE AND SCIENCE

"The world is my Idea"—This is a truth which holds good for everything that lives and knows, though man alone can bring it into reflective and abstract consciousness. If he really does this, he has attained to philosophical wisdom. It then becomes clear and certain to him that what he knows is not a sun and an earth, but only an eye that sees a sun, a hand that feels an earth; that the world which surrounds him is there only as idea, *i.e.*, only in relation to something else, the consciousness, which is himself. If any truth can be asserted *a priori*, it is this: for it is the expression of the most general form of all possible and thinkable experience:

a form which is more general than time, or space, or causality, for they all presuppose it; and each of these, which we have seen to be just so many modes of the principle of sufficient reason, is valid only for a particular class of ideas; whereas the antithesis of object and subject is the common form of all these classes, is that form under which alone any idea of whatever kind it may be, abstract or intuitive, pure or empirical, is possible and thinkable. No truth therefore is more certain, more independent of all others, and less in need of proof than this, that all that exists for knowledge, and therefore this whole world, is only object in relation to subject, perception of a perceiver, in a word, idea. This is obviously true of the past and the future, as well as of the present, of what is farthest off, as of what is near; for it is true of time and space themselves, in which alone these distinctions arise. All that in any way belongs or can belong to the world is inevitably thus conditioned through the subject, and exists only for the subject. The world is idea.

That which knows all things and is known by none is the subject. Thus it is the supporter of the world, that condition of all phenomena, of all objects which is always presupposed throughout experience; for all that exists, exists only for the subject. Everyone finds himself to be subject, yet only in so far as he knows, not in so far as he is an object of knowledge. But his body is object, and therefore from this point of view we call it idea. For the body is an object among objects, and is conditioned by the laws of objects, although it is an immediate object. Like all objects of perception, it lies within the universal forms of knowledge, time and space, which are the conditions of multiplicity. The subject, on the contrary, which is always the knower, never the known, does not come under these forms, but is presupposed by them; it has therefore neither multiplicity nor its opposite unity. We never know it, but it is always the knower wherever there is knowledge.

So then the world as idea, the only aspect in which we consider it at present, has two fundamental, necessary and inseparable halves. The one half is the object, the forms of which are space and time, and through these multiplicity. The other half is the subject, which is not in space and time, for it is present, entire and undivided, in every percipient being. So that any one percipient being, with the object, constitutes the whole world as idea just as fully as the existing millions could do; but if this one were to disappear, then the whole world as idea would cease to be.

On the one side realistic dogmatism, looking upon the idea as the effect of the object, desires to separate these two, idea and object, which are really one, and to assume a cause quite different from the idea, an object in itself, independent of the subject, a thing which is quite inconceivable; for even as object it presupposes subject, and so remains its idea. Opposed to this doctrine is scepticism, which makes the same false presupposition that in the idea we have only the effect, never the cause, therefore never real being; that we always know merely the action of the object. But this object, it supposes, may perhaps have no resemblance whatever to its effect, may

indeed have been quite erroneously received as the cause,
for the law of causality is first to be gathered from
experience, and the reality of experience is then made to
rest upon it. Thus both of these views are open to the
correction, firstly, that object and idea are the same;
secondly, that the true being of the object of perception is
its action, that the reality of the thing consists in this, and
the demand for an existence of the object outside the idea
of the subject, and also for an essence of the actual thing
different from its action, has absolutely no meaning, and
is a contradiction: and that the knowledge of the nature
of the effect of any perceived object, exhausts such an
object itself, so far as it is object, *i.e.*, idea, for beyond this
there is nothing more to be known. So far then, the
perceived world in space and time, which makes itself
known as causation alone is entirely real, and is
throughout simply what it appears to be, and it appears
wholly and without reserve as idea, bound together
according to the law of causality. This is its empirical
reality. On the other hand, and causality is in the
understanding alone, and for the understanding. The
whole actual, that is, active world is determined as such
through the understanding, and apart from it is nothing.
This, however, is not the only reason for altogether
denying such a reality of the outer world as is taught by
the dogmatist, who explains its reality as its independence
of the subject. We also deny it, because no object apart
from a subject can be conceived without contradiction.
The whole world of objects is and remains idea, and
therefore wholly and for ever determined by the subject;

that is to say, it has transcendental ideality. But it is not therefore illusion or mere appearance; it presents itself as that which it is, idea, and indeed as a series of ideas of which the common bond is the principle of sufficient reason. It is according to its inmost meaning quite comprehensible to the healthy understanding, and speaks a language quite intelligible to it. To dispute about its reality can only occur to a mind perverted by over-subtility, and such discussion always arises from a false application of the principle of sufficient reason, which binds all ideas together of whatever kind they may be, but by no means connects them with the subject, nor yet with a something which is neither subject or object but only the ground of the object; an absurdity, for only objects can be and always are the ground of objects.

So far as we have considered the question of the reality of the outer world, it arises from a confusion which amounts even to a misunderstanding of reason itself, and therefore thus far, the question could be answered only by explaining its meaning. After examination of the whole nature of the principle of sufficient reason, of the relation of subject and object, and the special conditions of sense perception, the question itself disappeared because it had no longer any meaning. There is, however, one other possible origin of this question, quite different from the purely speculative one which we have considered, a specially empirical origin, though the question is always raised from a speculative point of view, and in this form it has a much more comprehensible meaning than it had in the first. We have dreams; may not our whole life be a dream? Or more exactly: is there sure criterion of the distinction between dreams and reality? Between phantasms and real objects? The assertion that what is dreamt is less vivid and distinct than what we actually perceive is not to the point, because no one has ever been able to make a fair comparison of the two; for we can only compare the recollection of a dream with the present reality. Kant answers the question thus: "The connection of ideas among themselves, according to the law of causality, constitutes the difference between real life and dreams." But in dreams, as well as in real life, everything is connected individually at any rate, in accordance with the principle of sufficient reason in all its forms, and this connection is broken only between life and dreams, or between one dream and another. Kant's answer therefore could only run thus: the *long* dream (life) has throughout complete connection according to the principle of sufficient reason; it has not this connection, however, with *short* dreams, although each of these has in itself the same connection: the bridge is therefore broken between the former and the latter, and on this account we distinguish them.

But to institute an inquiry according to this criterion, as to whether something was dreamt or seen, would always be difficult and often impossible. For we are by no means in a position to trace link by link the causal connection between any experienced event and the present moment, but we do not on that account explain it as dreamt. Therefore in real life we do not commonly employ that method of distinguishing between dreams and reality. The only sure criterion by which to distinguish them is in fact the entirely empirical one of awaking, through which at any rate the causal connection between dreamed events and those of waking life, is distinctly and sensibly broken off. This is strongly supported by the remark of Hobbes in the second chapter of *Leviathan* that we easily mistake dreams for reality if we have unintentionally fallen asleep without taking off our clothes, and much more so when it also happens that some undertaking or design fills all our thoughts, and occupies our dreams as well as our waking moments. We then observe the awaking just as little as the falling asleep, dream and reality run together and become confounded. In such a case there is nothing for it but the application of Kant's criterion; but if, as often happens, we fail to establish by means of this criterion, either the existence of causal connection with the present, or the absence of such connection, then it must for ever remain uncertain whether an event was dreamt or really happened. Here, in fact, the intimate relationship between life and dreams is brought out very clearly, and we need not be ashamed to confess it, as it has been recognized and spoken of by many great men. The Vedas and Puranas have no better simile than a dream for the whole knowledge of the actual world, which they call the web of Maya, and they use none more frequently. Plato often says that men live only in a dream; the philosopher alone strives to awake himself. Pindar says (ii η. 135): σκιὰς ὄνάρ ὄᾳθωπος (umbræ somnium home), and Sophocles:

Ορῶ γὰρ ἡμὰς οὐδὲν ὄντας ἄλλο, πλὴν
εἴωλ ὄσοιπερ ζῶμεν, ἠκούρην σκιάν —Ajax, 125

(Nos enim, quicunque vivimus, nihil aliud esse comperio quam simulacra et levem umbram.) Beside which most worthily stands Shakespeare:

> "We are such stuff
> As dreams are made on, and our little life
> Is rounded with a sleep."—*Tempest*, Act IV. Sc. i.

Lastly, Calderon was so deeply impressed with this view of life that he sought to embody it in a kind of metaphysical drama—"Life a Dream."

After these numerous quotations from the poets, perhaps I also may be allowed to express myself by a metaphor. Life and dreams are leaves of the same book. The systematic reading of this book is real life, but when the reading hours (that is, the day) are over, we often continue idly to turn over the leaves, and read a page here and there without method or connection: often one we have read before, sometimes one that is new to us, but always in the same book. Such an isolated page is indeed out of connection with the systematic study of the book, but it does not seem so very different when we remember that the whole continuous perusal begins and ends just as abruptly, and may therefore be regarded as merely a larger single page.

Understanding is the same in all animals and in all men; it has everywhere the same simple form; knowledge of causality, transition from effect to cause, and from cause to effect, nothing more; but the degree of its acuteness, and the extension of the sphere of its knowledge varies enormously, with innumerable gradations from the lowest form, which is only conscious of the causal connection between the immediate object and objects affecting it—that is to say, perceives a cause as an object in space by passing to it from the affection which the body feels, to the higher grades of knowledge of the causal connection among objects known indirectly, which extends to the understanding of the most complicated system of cause and effect in nature. For even this high degree of knowledge is still the work of the understanding, not of the reason. The abstract concepts of the reason can only serve to take up the objective connections which are immediately known by the understanding, to make them permanent for thought, and to relate them to each other; but reason never gives us immediate knowledge. Every force and law of Nature, every example of such forces and laws, must first be immediately known by the understanding, must be apprehended through perception before it can pass into abstract consciousness for reason.

The understanding has only one function—immediate knowledge of the relation of cause and effect. Yet the perception of the real world, and all common sense, sagacity and inventiveness, however multifarious their applications may be, are quite clearly seen to be nothing more than manifestations of that one function. So also the reason has one function; and from it all the manifestations of reason we have mentioned, which distinguish the life of man from that of the brutes, may easily be explained.

The application or the non-application of this function is all that is meant by what men have everywhere and always called rational and irrational.

❖

Second Book
The World As Will

First Aspect

The Objectification of the will

he science of mechanics presupposes matter, weight, impenetrability, the possibility of communicating motion by impact, inertia and so forth as ultimate facts, calls them forces of nature, and their necessary and orderly appearance under certain conditions a law of nature. Only after this does its explanation begin, and it consists in indication truly and with mathematical exactness, how, where and when each force manifests itself, and in referring every phenomenon which presents itself to the operation of one of these forces. Physics, chemistry and physiology proceed in the same way in their province, only they presuppose more and accomplish less. The causal connection merely gives us the rule and the relative order of their appearance in space and time, but affords us no further knowledge of that which so appears. Moreover, the law of causality itself has only validity for ideas, for objects of a definite class, and it has meaning only in so far as it presupposes them. Thus, like these objects themselves, it always exists only in relation to a subject, that is, conditionally; and so it is known just as well if we start from the subject, *i.e., a priori*, as if we start from the object, *i.e., a posteriori*. Kant indeed has taught us this.

But what now impels us to inquiry is just that we are not satisfied with knowing that we have ideas, that they are such and such, and that they are connected according to certain laws, the general expression of which is the principle of sufficient reason. We wish to know the significance of these ideas; we ask whether this world is merely idea; in which case it would pass by us like an empty dream or a baseless vision, not worth our notice; or whether it is also something else, something more than idea, and if so, what. Thus much is certain, that this something we seek for must be completely and in its whole nature different from the idea; that the forms and laws of the idea must therefore be completely foreign to it; further, that we cannot arrive at it from the idea under the guidance of the laws which merely combine objects, ideas, among themselves, and which are the forms of the principle of sufficient reason.

Thus we see already that we can never arrive at the real nature of things from without. However much we investigate, we can never reach anything but images and names. We are like a man who goes round a castle seeking in vain for an entrance, and sometimes sketching the façades. An yet this is the method that has been followed by all philosophers before me.

In fact, the meaning for which we seek of that world which is present to us only as our idea, or the transition from the world as mere idea of the knowing subject to whatever it may be besides this, would never be found if the investigator himself were nothing more than the pure knowing subject (a winged cherub without a body). But he is himself rooted in that world; he finds himself in it as an *individual*, that is to say, his knowledge, which is the necessary supporter of the whole world as idea, is yet always given through the medium of a body, whose affections are, as we have shown, the starting-point for the understanding in the perception of that world. His body is, for the pure knowing subject, an idea like every other idea, an object among objects. Its movements and actions are so far known to him in precisely the same way as the changes of all other perceived objects, and would be just as strange and incomprehensible to him if their meaning were not explained for him in an entirely different way. Otherwise he would see his actions follow upon given motives with the constancy of a law of nature, just as the changes of other objects follow upon causes, stimuli or motives. But he would not understand the influence of the motives any more than the connection between every other effect which he sees and its cause. He would then

call the inner nature of these manifestations and actions
of his body which he did not understand a force, a quality
or a character, as he pleased, but he would have no further
insight into it. But all this is not the case; indeed the
answer to the riddle is given to the subject of knowledge
who appears as an individual, and the answer is *will*. This
and this alone gives him the key to his own existence,
reveals to him the significance, shows him the inner
mechanism of his being, of his action, of his movements.
The body is given in two entirely different ways to the
subject of knowledge, who becomes an individual only
through his identity with it. It is given as an idea in
intelligent perception, as an object among objects and
subject to the laws of objects. And it is also given in quite
a different way as that which is immediately known to
everyone, and is signified by the word *will*. Every true act
of his will is also at once and without exception a
movement of his body. The act of will and the movement
of the body are not two different things objectively known,
which the bond of causality unites; they do not stand in
the relation of cause and effect; they are one and the same;
but they are given in entirely different ways—immediately,
and again in perception for the understanding. The action
of the body is nothing but the act of the will objectified,
i.e., passed into perception. It will appear later that this
is true of every movement of the body, not merely those
which follow upon motives, but also involuntary
movements which follow upon mere stimuli, and, indeed,
that the whole body is nothing but objectified will, *i.e.,* will
become idea. All this will be proved and made quite clear

in the course of this work. In one respect, therefore, I shall call the body the *objectivity of will*; as in the previous book, and in the essay on the principle of sufficient reason, in accordance with the one-sided point of view intentionally adopted there (that of the idea), I called it *the immediate object*. It is just because of this special relation to one body that the knowing subject is an individual. For regarded apart from this relation, his body is for him only an idea like all other ideas. But the relation through which the knowing subject is an *individual*, is just on that account a relation which subsists only between him and one particular idea of all those which he has. Therefore he is conscious of this one idea, not merely as an idea, but in quite a different way as a will. If, however, he abstracts from that special relation, from that twofold and completely heterogeneous knowledge of what is one and the same, then that *one*, the body, is an idea like all other ideas. Therefore, in order to understand the matter, the individual who knows must either assume that what distinguishes that one idea from others is merely the fact that his knowledge stands in this double relation to it alone; that insight in two ways at the same time is open to him only in the case of this one object of perception, and that this is to be explained not by the difference of this object from all others, but only by the difference between the relation of his knowledge to this one object, and its relation to all other objects. Or else he must assume that this object is essentially different from all others; that it alone of all objects is at once both will and idea, while the rest are only ideas, *i.e.,* only phantoms. Thus he must assume that his body is the only real individual in the world, *i.e.*, the only phenomenon of will and the only immediate object of the subject. That other objects, considered merely as *ideas*, are like his body, that is, like it, fill space (which itself can only be present as idea), and also, like it, are causally active in space, is indeed \demonstrably certain from the law of causality which is *a priori* valid for ideas, and which admits of no effect without a cause; but apart from the fact that we can only reason from an effect to a cause generally, and not to a similar cause, we are still in the sphere of mere ideas, in which alone the law of causality is valid, and beyond which it can never take us. But whether the objects known to the individual only as ideas are yet, like his own body, manifestations of a will, is, as was said in the First Book, the proper meaning of the question as to the reality of the external world. To deny this is *theoretical egoism*, which on that account regards all phenomena that are outside its own will as phantoms, just as in a practical reference exactly the same thing is done by practical egoism. For in it a man regards and treats himself alone as a person, and all other persons as mere phantoms. Theoretical egoism can never be demonstrably refuted, yet in philosophy it has never been used otherwise than as a sceptical sophism, *i.e.*, a pretence. As a serious conviction, on the other hand, it could only be found in a madhouse, and as such it stands in need of a cure rather than a refutation. We do not therefore combat it any further in this regard, but treat it as merely the last stronghold of scepticism, which is always polemical. Thus our knowledge, which is always bound to individuality and is limited by this circumstance, brings with it the necessity that each of us can only *be one*, while, on the other hand, each of us can *know all;* and it is this limitation that creates the need for philosophy. We therefore who, for this very reason, are striving to extend the limits of our knowledge through philosophy, will treat this sceptical argument of theoretical egoism which meets us, as an army would treat a small frontier fortress. The fortress cannot indeed be taken, but the garrison can never sally forth from it, and therefore we pass it by without danger, and are not afraid to have it in our rear.

As we have said, the will proclaims itself primarily in the voluntary movements of our own body, as the inmost nature of this body, as that which it is besides being object of perception, idea. For these voluntary movements are nothing else than the visible aspect of the individual acts of will, with which they are directly coincident and identical, and only distinguished through the form of knowledge into which they have passed, and in which alone they can be known, the form of idea.

But these acts of will have always a ground or reason outside themselves in motives. Yet these motives never determine more than that I will at *this* time, in *this* place, and under *these* circumstances, not *that* I will in general, or *what* I will in general, that is, the maxims which characterize my volition generally. Therefore the inner nature of my volition cannot be explained from these motives; but they merely determine its manifestation at a given point of time: they are merely the occasion of my will showing itself; but the will itself lies outside the province of the law of motivation, which determines nothing but its appearance at each point of time. It is only under the presupposition of my empirical character that the motive is a sufficient ground of explanation of my action. But if I abstract from my character, and then ask, why, in general, I will this and not that, no answer is possible, because it is only the manifestation of the will that is subject to the principle of sufficient reason, and not the will itself, which in this respect is to be called *groundless*. For the present, I have to draw attention to this, that the fact of one manifestation being established through another, as here the deed through the motive, does not at all conflict with the fact that its real nature is will, which itself has no *ground;* for as the principle of sufficient reason in all its aspects is only the form of knowledge, its validity extends only to the idea, to the phenomena, to the visibility of the will, but not to the will itself, which becomes visible.

If now every action of my body is the manifestation of an act of will in which my will itself in general, and as a whole, thus my character, expresses itself under given motives, manifestation of the will must be the inevitable condition and presupposition of every action. For the fact of its manifestation cannot depend upon something which does not exist directly and only through it, which consequently is for it merely accidental, and through which its manifestation itself would be merely accidental. Now that condition is just the whole body itself. Thus the body itself must be manifestation of the will, and it must be related to my will as a whole, that is, to my intelligible character, whose phenomenal appearance in time is my empirical character, as the particular action of the body is related to the particular act of the will. The whole body, then must be simply my will become visible, must be my will itself, so far as this is object of perception, an idea of the first class. Indeed we can also give an etiological account, though a very incomplete one, of the origin of my body, and a somewhat better account of its development and conservation, and this is the substance of physiology. Even supposing it really could give a thorough explanation of this kind, yet this would never invalidate the immediately certain truth that every voluntary motion (*functiones animales*) is the manifestation of an act of will. Now, just as little can the physiological explanation of vegetative life (*functiones naturales vitales*), however far it may advance, ever invalidate the truth that the whole animal life which thus develops itself is the manifestation of will. In general, then, as we have shown above, no etiological explanation can ever give us more than the necessarily determined position in time and space of a particular manifestation, its necessary appearance there, according to a fixed law; but the inner nature of everything that appears in this way remains wholly inexplicable, and is presupposed by every etiological explanation, and merely indicated by the names, force, or law of Nature, or, if we are speaking of action, character or will. Thus, although every particular action, under the presupposition of the definite character, necessarily follows from the given motive, and although growth, the process of nourishment, and all the changes of the animal body take place according to necessarily acting causes (stimuli), yet the whole series of actions, and consequently every individual act, and also its condition, the whole body itself which accomplishes it, and therefore also the process through which and in which it exists, are nothing but the manifestation of the will, the becoming visible, *the objectification of the will.* Upon this rests the perfect suitableness of the human and animal body to the human and animal will in general, resembling, though far surpassing, the correspondence between an instrument made for a purpose and the will of the maker, and on this account appearing as design, *i.e.,* the teleological explanation of the body. The parts of the body must, therefore, completely correspond to the principal desires through which the will manifests itself; they must be the visible expression of these desires. Teeth, throat, and bowels are objectified hunger; the organs of generation are objectified sexual desire; the grasping hand, the hurrying feet, correspond to the more indirect desires of the will which they express. As the human form generally corresponds to the human will generally, so the individual bodily structure corresponds to the individually modified will, the character of the individual, and therefore it is throughout and in all its parts characteristic and full of expression.

Whoever has now gained from all these expositions a knowledge *in abstracto*, and therefore clear and certain, of what everyone knows directly *in concreto, i.e.,* as feeling, a knowledge that his will is the real inner nature of his phenomenal being, which manifests itself to him as idea, both in his actions and in their permanent substratum, his body, and that his will is that which is most immediate in his consciousness, though it has not as such completely passed into the form of idea in which object and subject stand over against each other, but makes itself known to him in a direct manner, in which he does not quite clearly distinguish subject and object, yet is not known as a whole to the individual himself, but only in its particular acts— whoever, I say, has with me gained this conviction will find that of itself it affords him the key to the knowledge of the inmost being of the whole of nature; for he now transfers it to all those phenomena which are not given to him, like his own phenomenal existence, both in direct and indirect knowledge, but only in the latter, thus merely one-sidedly as *idea* alone. He will recognize this will of which we are speaking not only in those phenomenal existences which exactly resemble his own, in men and animals as their inmost nature, but the course of reflection will lead him to recognize the force which germinates and vegetates in the plant, and indeed the force through which the crystal is formed, that by which the magnet turns to the north pole, the force whose shock he experiences from the contact of two different kinds of metals, the force which appears in the elective affinities of matter as repulsion and attraction, decomposition and combination, and, lastly, even gravitation, which acts so powerfully throughout matter, draws the stone to the earth and the earth to the sun—all these, I say, he will recognize as different only in their phenomenal existence, but in their inner nature as identical, as that which is directly known to him so intimately and so much better than anything else, and which in its most distinct manifestation is called *will*. It is this application of reflection alone that prevents us from remaining any longer at the phenomenon, and leads us to the *thing in itself.* Phenomenal existence is idea and nothing more. All idea, of whatever kind it may be, all *object*, is *phenomenal* existence, but the *will* alone is a *thing in itself.* As such, it is throughout not idea, but *toto genere* different from it; it is that of which all idea, all object, is the phenomenal appearance, the visibility, the objectification. It is the inmost nature, the kernel, of every particular thing, and also of the whole. It appears in every blind force of Nature and also in the preconsidered action of man; and the great difference between these two is merely in the degree of the manifestation, not in the nature of what manifests itself.

It is, however, well to observe that here, at any rate, we only make use of a *denomination a potiori*, through which, therefore, the concept of will receives a greater extension than it has hitherto had. Knowledge of the identical in different phenomena, and of difference in similar phenomena, is, as Plato so often remarks, a *sine qua non* of philosophy. But hitherto it was not recognized that every kind of active and operating force in Nature is essentially identical with will, and therefore the multifarious kinds of phenomena were not seen to be merely different species of the same genus, but were treated as heterogeneous. Consequently there could be no word to denote the concept of this genus. I therefore name the genus after its most important species, the direct knowledge of which lies nearer to us and guides us to indirect knowledge of all other species. But whoever is incapable of carrying out the required extension of the concept will remain involved in *r* permanent misunderstanding. For by the word *will* he understands only that species of it which has hitherto been exclusively denoted by it, the will which is guided by knowledge, and whose manifestation follows only upon motives, and indeed merely abstract motives, and thus take place under the guidance of the reason. This, we have said, is only the most prominent example of the manifestation of will. We must now distinctly separate in thought the inmost essence of this manifestation which is known to us directly, and then transfer it to all the weaker, less distinct manifestations of the same nature, and thus we shall accomplish the desired extension of the concept of will.

The *will* as a thing in itself is quite different form its phenomenal appearance, and entirely free from all the forms of the phenomenal, into which it first passes when it manifests itself, and which therefore only concern its *objectivity*, and are foreign to the will itself. Even the most universal form of all idea, that of being object for a subject, does not concern it; still less the forms which are subordinate to this and which collectively have their common expression in the principle of sufficient reason, to which we know that time and space belong, and consequently multiplicity also, which exists and is possible only through these. In this last regard I shall call time and space the *principium individuationis*, borrowing an expression from the old schoolmen, and I beg to draw attention to this, once for all. For it is only through the medium of time and space that what is one and the same, both according to its nature and to its concept, yet appears as different, as a multiplicity of co-existent and successive phenomena. Thus time and space are the *principium individuationis*, the subject of so many subtleties and disputes among the schoolmen, which may be found collected in Suarez (Disp. 5, Sect. 3). According to what has been said, the will as a thing-in-itself lies outside the province of the principle of sufficient reason in all its forms, and is consequently completely groundless, although all its manifestations are entirely subordinated to the principle of sufficient reason. Further, it is free from all *multiplicity*, although its manifestations in time and space are innumerable. It is itself one, though not in the sense in which an object is one, for the unity of an object can only be known in opposition to a possible multiplicity; nor yet in the sense in which a concept is one, for the unity of a concept originates only in abstraction from a multiplicity; but it is one as that which lies outside time and space, the *principium individuationis*, *i.e.*, the possibility of multiplicity. Only when all this has become quite clear to us through the subsequent examination of the phenomena and different manifestations of the will, shall we fully understand the meaning of the Kantian doctrine that time, space and causality do not belong to the thing-in-itself, but are only forms of knowing.

The uncaused nature of will has been actually recognized, where it manifests itself most distinctly, as the will of man, and this has been called free, independent. But on account of the uncaused nature of the will itself, the necessity to which its manifestation is everywhere subjected has been overlooked, and actions are treated as free, which they are not. For every individual action follows with strict necessity from the effect of the motive upon the character. All necessity is, as we have already said, the relation of the consequent to the reason, and nothing more. The principle of sufficient reason is the universal form of all phenomena, and man in his action must be subordinated to it like every other phenomenon. But because in self-consciousness the will is known directly and in itself, in this consciousness lies also the consciousness of freedom. The fact is, however, overlooked that the individual, the person, is not will as a thing-in-itself, but is a *phenomenon* of will, is already determined as such, and has come under the form of the phenomenal, the principle of sufficient reason. Hence arises the strange fact that everyone believes himself *a priori* to be perfectly free, even in his individual actions, and thinks that at every moment he can commence another manner of life, which just means that he can become another person. But *a posteriori*, through experience, he finds to his astonishment that he is not free, but subjected to necessity; that in spite of all his resolutions and reflections he does not change his conduct, and that from the beginning of his life to the end of it, he must carry out the very character which he himself condemns, and as it were play the part he has undertaken to the end. I cannot pursue this subject further at present, for it belongs, as ethical, to another part of this work. In the meantime, I only wish to point out here that the *phenomenon* of the will which in itself is uncaused, is yet as such subordinated to the law of necessity, that is, the principle of sufficient reason, so that in the necessity with which the phenomena of Nature follow each other, we may find nothing to hinder us from recognizing in them the manifestations of will.

Only those changes which have no other ground than a motive, *i.e.*, an idea, have hitherto been regarded as manifestations of will. Therefore in Nature a will has only been attributed to man, or at the most to animals; for knowledge, the idea is, of course, as I have said elsewhere, the true and exclusive characteristic of animal life. But that the will is also active where no knowledge guides it, we see at once in the instinct and the mechanical skill of animals. That they have ideas and knowledge is here not to the point, for the end towards which they strive as definitely as if it were a known motive, is yet entirely unknown to them. Therefore in such cases their action takes place without motive, is not guided by the idea, and shows us first and most distinctly how the will may be active entirely without knowledge. The bird of a year old has no idea of the eggs for which it builds a nest; the young spider has no idea of the prey for which it spins a web; nor has the ant-lion any idea of the ants for which he digs a trench for the first time. The larva of the stag-beetle makes the hole in the wood, in which it is to await its metamorphosis, twice as big if it is going to be a male beetle as if it is going to be a female, so that if it is a male there may be room for the horns of which, however, it has no idea. In such actions of these creatures the will is clearly operative as in their other actions, but it is in blind activity, which is indeed accompanied by knowledge but not guided by it. If now we have once gained insight into the fact that idea as motive is not a necessary and essential condition of the activity of the will, we shall more easily recognize the activity of will where it is less apparent. For example, we shall see that the house of the snail is no more made by a will which is foreign to the snail itself, than the house which we build is produced through another will than our own; but we shall recognize in both houses the work of a will which objectifies itself in both the phenomena—a will which works in us according to motives, but in the snail still blindly as formative impulse directed outwards. In us also the same will is in many ways only blindly active: in all the functions of our body which are not guided by knowledge, in all its vital and vegetative processes, digestion, circulation, secretion, growth, reproduction. Not only the actions of the body, but the whole body itself is, we have shown above, phenomenon of the will, objectified will, concrete will. All that goes on in it must therefore proceed through will, although here this will is not guided by knowledge, but acts blindly according to causes, which in this case are called *stimuli*.

It only remains for us to take the final step, the extension of our way of looking at things to all those forces which act in nature in accordance with universal, unchangeable laws, in conformity with which the movements of all those bodies take place, which are wholly without organs, and have therefore no susceptibility for stimuli, and have no knowledge, which is the necessary condition of motives. Thus we must also apply the key to the understanding of the inner nature of things, which the immediate knowledge of our own existence alone can give us, to those phenomena of the unorganized world which are most remote from us. And if we consider them attentively, if we observe the strong and unceasing impulse with which the waters hurry to the ocean, the persistency with which the magnet turns ever to the North Pole, the readiness with which the electric poles seek to be re-united, and which, just like human desire, is increased by obstacles; if we see the crystal quickly and suddenly take form with such wonderful regularity of construction, which is clearly only a perfectly definite and accurately determined impulse in different directions, seized and retained by crystalization; if we observe the choice with which bodies repel and attract each other, combine and separate, when they are set free in a fluid state, and emancipated from the bonds of rigidness; lastly, if we feel directly how a burden which hampers our body by its gravitation towards the earth, unceasingly presses and strains upon it in pursuit of its one tendency; if we observe all this, I say, it will require no great effort of the imagination to recognize, even at so great a distance, our own nature. That which in us pursues its ends by the light of knowledge; but here, in the weakest of its manifestations, only strives blindly and dumbly in a one-sided and unchangeable manner, must yet in both cases come under the name of will, as it is everywhere one and the same—just as the first dim light of dawn must share the name of sunlight with the rays of the full midday. For the name *will* denotes that which is the inner nature of everything in the world, and the one kernel of every phenomenon.

Yet the remoteness, and indeed the appearance of absolute difference between the phenomena of unorganized nature and the will which we know as the inner reality of our own being, arises chiefly from the contrast between the completely determined conformity to law of the one species of phenomena, and the apparently unfettered freedom of the other. For in man, individuality makes itself powerfully felt. Everyone has a character of his own; and therefore the same motive has not the same influence over all, and a thousand circumstances which exist in the wide sphere of the knowledge of the individual, but are unknown to others, modify its effect. Therefore action cannot be predetermined from the motive alone, for the other factor is wanting, the accurate acquaintance with the individual character, and with the knowledge which accompanies it. On the other hand, the phenomena of the forces of nature illustrate the opposite extreme. They act according to universal laws, without variation, without individuality in accordance with openly manifest circumstances, subject to the most exact predetermination;

and the same force of Nature appears in its million phenomena in precisely the same way.

❖

We know the *multiplicity* in general is necessarily conditioned by space and time, and is only thinkable in them. In this respect they are called the *principium individuationis*. But we have found that space and time are forms of the principle of sufficient reason. In this principle all our knowledge *a priori* is expressed, but, as we showed above, this a *priori* knowledge, as such, only applies to the knowableness of things, not to the things themselves, *i.e.*, it is only our form of knowledge, it is not a property of the thing-in-itself. The thing-in-itself is, as such, free from all forms of knowledge, even the most universal, that of being an object for the subject. In other words, the thing-in-itself is something altogether different from the idea. If, now, this thing-in-itself is *the will*, as I believe I have fully and convincingly proved it to be, then, regarded as such and apart from its manifestation, it lies outside time and space, and therefore knows no multiplicity, and is consequently *one*. Yet as I have said, it is not one in the sense in which an individual or a concept is one, but as something to which the condition of the possibility of multiplicity, the *principium individuationis*, is foreign. The multiplicity of things in space and time, which collectively constitute the objectification of will, does not affect the will itself, which remains indivisible notwithstanding it. It is not the case that, in some way or other, a smaller part of will is in the stone and a larger part in the man, for the relation of part and whole belongs exclusively to space, and has no longer any meaning when we go beyond this form of intuition or perception. The more and the less have application only to the phenomenon of will, that is, its visibility, its objectification. Of this there is a higher grade in the plant than in the stone; in the animal a higher grade than in the plant: indeed, the passage of will into visibility, its objectification, has grades as innumerable as exist between the dimmest twilight and the brightest sunshine, the loudest sound and the faintest echo. We shall return later to the consideration of these grades of visibility which belong to the objectification of the will, to the reflection of its nature. But as the grades of its objectification do not directly concern the will itself, still less is it concerned by the multiplicity of the phenomena of these different grades, *i.e.*, the multitude of individuals of each form, or the particular manifestations of each force. For this multiplicity is directly conditioned by time and space, into which the will itself never enters. The will reveals itself as completely and as much in *one* oak as in millions. Their number and multiplication in space and time has no meaning with regard to it, but only with regard to the multiplicity of individuals who know in space and time, and who are themselves multiplied and dispersed in these. The multiplicity of these individuals itself belongs not to the will, but only to its manifestation. We may therefore say that if, *per impossibile*, a single real existence, even the most insignificant, were to be entirely annihilated, the whole world would necessarily perish with it.

❖

The lowest grades of the objectification of will are to be found in those most universal forces of Nature which partly appear in all matter without exception, as gravity and impenetrability, and partly have shared the given matter among them, so that certain of them reign in one species of matter and others in another species, constituting its specific difference, as rigidity, fluidity, elasticity, electricity, magnetism, chemical properties and qualities of every kind. They are in themselves immediate manifestations of will, just as much as human action; and as such they are groundless, like human character. Only their particular manifestations are subordinated to the principle of sufficient reason, like the particular actions of men. They themselves, on the other hand, can never be called either effect or cause, but are the prior and presupposed conditions of all causes and effects through which their real nature unfolds and reveals itself. It is therefore senseless to demand a cause of gravity or electricity, for they are original forces. Their expressions, indeed, take place in accordance with the law of cause and effect, so that every one of their particular manifestations has a cause, which is itself again just a similar particular manifestation which determines that this force must express itself here, must appear in space and time; but the force itself is by no means the effect of a cause, nor the cause of an effect. It is therefore a mistake to say "gravity is the cause of a stone falling"; for he cause in this case is rather the nearness of the earth, because it attracts the stone. Take the earth away and the stone will not fall, although gravity remains. The force itself lies quite outside the chain of causes and effects, which presupposes time, because it only has meaning in relation to it; but the force lies outside time. The individual change always has for its cause another change just as individual as itself, and not the force of which it is the expression. For that which always gives its efficiency to a cause, however many times it may appear, is a force of Nature. As such, it is groundless, *i.e.*, it lies outside the chain of causes and outside the province of the principle of sufficient reason in general, and is philosophically known as the immediate objectivity of will, which is the "in-itself" of the whole of Nature; but in etiology, which in this reference is physics, it is set down as an original force, *i.e.*, a *qualitas occulta*.

In the higher grades of the objectivity of will we see individuality occupy a prominent position, especially in the case of man, where it appears as the great difference of individual characters, *i.e.*, as complete personality, outwardly expressed in strongly marked individual physiognomy, which influences the whole bodily form. None of the brutes have this individuality in anything like so high a degree, though the higher species of them have a trace of it; but the character of the species completely predominates over it, and therefore they have little individual physiognomy. The farther down we go, the more completely is every trace of the individual character lost in the common character of the species, and the physiognomy of the species alone remains. We know the physiological character of the species, and from that we know exactly what is to be expected from the individual; while, on the contrary, in the human species every individual has to be studied and fathomed for himself, which, if we wish to forecast his action with some degree of certainty, is, on account of the possibility of concealment that first appears with reason, a matter of the greatest difficulty. It is probably connected with this difference of the human species from all others, that the folds and convolutions of the brain, which are entirely wanting in birds, and very weakly marked in rodents, are even in the case of the higher animals far more symmetrical on both sides, and more constantly the same in each individual, than in the case of human beings. It is further to be regarded as a phenomenon of this peculiar individual character which distinguishes men from all the lower animals, that in the case of the brutes the sexual instinct seeks its satisfaction without observable choice of objects, while in the case of man this choice is, in a purely instinctive manner and independent of all reflection, carried so far that it rises into a powerful passion. While then every man is to be regarded as a specially determined and characterized phenomenon of will, and indeed to a certain extent as a special Idea, in the case of the brutes this individual character as a whole is wanting, because only the species has a special significance. And the farther we go from man, the fainter becomes the trace of this individual character, so that plants have no individual qualities left, except such as may be fully explained from the favourable or unfavourable external influences of soil, climate and other accidents. Finally, in the inorganic kingdom of Nature all individuality disappears.

Every universal, original force of Nature is nothing but

a low grade of the objectification of will, and we call every such grade an eternal *idea* in Plato's sense. But a *law of nature* is the relation of the Idea to the form of its manifestation. This form is time, space and causality, which are necessarily and inseparably connected and related to each other. Through time and space the Idea multiplies itself in innumerable phenomena, but the order according to which it enters these forms of multiplicity is definitely determined by the law of causality; this law is as it were the norm of the limit of these phenomena of different Ideas, in accordance with which time, space and matter are assigned to them. This norm is therefore necessarily related to the identity of the aggregate of existing matter, which is the common substratum of all those different phenomena.

The magnet that has attracted a piece of iron carries on a perpetual conflict with gravitation, which, as the lower objectification of will, has a prior right to the matter of the iron; and in this constant battle the magnet indeed grows stronger, for the opposition excites it, as it were, to greater effort. In the same way every manifestation of the will, including that which expresses itself in the human organism, wages a constant war against the many physical and chemical forces which, as lower Ideas, have a prior right to that matter. Thus the arm falls which for a while, overcoming gravity, we have held stretched out; thus the pleasing sensation of health, which proclaims the victory of the Idea of the self-conscious organism over the physical

and chemical laws, which originally governed the
humours of the body, is so often interrupted, and is indeed
always accompanied by greater or less discomfort, which
arises from the resistance of these forces, and on account
of which the vegetative part of our life is constantly
attended by slight pain. Thus also indigestion weakens all
the animal functions, because it requires the whole vital
force to overcome the chemical forces of Nature by
assimilation. Hence also in general the burden of physical
life, the necessity of sleep, and, finally of death; for at last
these subdued forces of nature, assisted by circumstances,
win back from the organism, wearied even by the constant
victory, the matter it took from them, and attain to an
unimpeded expression of their being. We may therefore
say that every organism expresses the Idea of which it is
the image, only after we have subtracted the part of its
force which is expended in subduing the lower Ideas that
strive with it for matter. This seems to have been running
in the mind of Jacob Böhme when he says somewhere that
all the bodies of men and animals, and even all plants, are
really half dead. According as the subjection in the
organism of these forces of Nature, which express the
lower grades of the objectivation of will, is more or less
successful, the more or the less completely does it attain
to the expression of its Idea; that is to say, the nearer it
is to the *ideal* or the farther from it—the *ideal* of beauty
in its species.

Thus everywhere in Nature we see strife, conflict and
alternation of victory, and in it we shall come to recognize
more distinctly that variance with itself which is essential

to the will. Every grade of the objectification of will fights for the matter, the space and the time of the others. The permanent matter must constantly change its form; from under the guidance of causality, mechanical, physical, chemical and organic phenomena, eagerly striving to appear, wrest the matter from each other, for each desires to reveal its own Idea. This strife may be followed through the whole of nature; indeed nature exists only through it: εἰ γὰρ μὴ ἦν τὸ νεῖκος τράγμασν, ἕν ἄν ἦν ἄπαντρ ὡς φησὶν Ἐμπεδοκλῆς (nam si non inesset in rebus contentio, unum omnia esent, ut ait Empedocles. Aris. *Metaph.*, B. 5). Yet this strife itself is only the revelation of that variance with itself which is essential to the will. This universal conflict becomes most distinctly visible in the animal kingdom. For animals have the whole of the vegetable kingdom for their food, and even within the animal kingdom every beast is the prey and the food of another; that is, the matter in which its Idea expresses itself must yield itself to the expression of another Idea, for each animal can only maintain its existence by the constant destruction of some other. Thus the will to live everywhere preys upon itself, and in different forms is its own nourishment, till finally the human race, because it subdues all the others, regards Nature as a manufactory for its use. Yet even the human race, as we shall see in the Fourth Book, reveals in itself with most terrible distinctness this conflict, this variance with itself of the will, and we find *homo homini lupus*. Meanwhile we can recognize this strife, this subjugation, just as well in the lower grades of the objectification of will. Many insects (especially ichneumon-flies) lay their eggs on the skin, and even in the body of the larvæ of other insects, whose slow destruction is the first work of the newly hatched brood. The young hydra, which grows like a bud out of the old one, and afterwards separates itself from it, fights while it is still joined to the old one for the prey that offers itself, so that the one snatches it out of the mouth of the other (Trembley, *Polypod.*, ii. p.110, and iii. p.165). But the bulldog-ant of Australia affords us the most extraordinary example of this kind; for if it is cut in two, a battle begins between the head and the tail. The head seizes the tail with its teeth, and the tail defends itself bravely by stinging the head: the battle may last for half an hour, until they die or are dragged away by other ants. This contest takes place every time the experiment is tried. (From a letter by Howitt in the W. Journal, reprinted in *Galignani's Messenger*, 17th November 1855.) On the banks of the Missouri one sometimes sees a mighty oak, the stem and branches of which are so encircled, fettered and interlaced by a gigantic wild vine, that it withers as if choked. The same thing shows itself in the lowest grades; for example, when water and carbon are changed into vegetable sap, or vegetables or bread into blood by organic assimilation; and so also in very case in which animal secretion takes place, along with the restriction of chemical forces to a subordinate mode of activity. On a large scale it shows itself in the relation between the central body and the planet, for although the planet is in absolute dependence, yet it always resists, just like the chemical forces in the organism; hence arises the constant tension between centripetal and centrifugal force, which keeps the globe in motion, and is itself an example of that universal essential conflict of the manifestation of will which we are considering. For as everybody must be regarded as the manifestation of a will, and as will necessarily expresses itself as a struggle, the original condition of every world that is formed into a globe cannot be rest, but motion, a striving forward in boundless space without rest and without end. Neither the law of inertia nor that of causality is opposed to this: for as, according to the former, matter as such is alike indifferent to rest and motion, its original condition may just as well be the one as the other, therefore if we first find it in motion, we have just as little right to assume that this was preceded by a condition of rest, and to inquire into the cause of the origin of the motion, as, conversely, if we found it at rest, we would have to assume a previous motion and inquire into the cause of its suspension. It is, therefore, not needful to seek for a first impulse for centrifugal force, for, according to the hypothesis of Kant and Laplace, it is, in the case of the planets, the residue of the original rotation of the central body, from which the planets have separated themselves as it contracted. But to this central body itself motion is essential; it always continues its rotation, and at the same time rushes forward in endless space, or perhaps circulates round a greater central body invisible to us. This view entirely agrees with the conjecture of astronomers that there is a central sun, and also with the observed advance of our whole solar system, and perhaps of the whole stellar system to which our sun belongs. From this we are finally led to assume a general advance of fixed stars, together with the central sun, and this certainly loses all meaning in boundless space (for motion in absolute space cannot be distinguished from rest), and becomes, as is already the case from its striving and aimless flight, an expression of that nothingness, that failure of all aim, which, at the close of this book we shall be obliged to recognize in the striving of will in all its phenomena. Thus boundless space and endless time must be the most universal and essential forms of the collective phenomena of will, which exist for the expression of its whole being.

Thus knowledge generally, rational as well as merely sensuous, proceeds originally from the will itself, belongs to the inner being of the higher grades of its objectification as a mere μηχανή, a means of supporting the individual and the species, just like any organ of the body. Originally destined for the service of the will for the accomplishment of its aims, it remains almost throughout entirely subjected to its service: it is so in all brutes and in almost all men. Yet we shall see in the Third Book how in certain individual men knowledge can deliver itself from this bondage, throw off its yoke, and, free from all the aims of will, exist purely for itself, simply as a clear mirror of the world, which is the source of art. Finally, in the Fourth Book, we shall see how, if this kind of knowledge reacts on the will, it can bring about self-surrender, *i.e.,* resignation, which is the final goal, and indeed the inmost nature of all virtue and holiness, and is deliverance from the world.

❖

Every will is a will towards something, has an object, an end of its willing; what then is the final end, or towards what is that will striving that is exhibited to us as the being-in-itself of the world? This question rests, like so many others, upon the confusion of the thing-in-itself with the manifestation. The principle of sufficient reason, of which the law of motivation is also a form, extends only to the latter, not to the former. It is only of phenomena, of individual things, that a ground can be given, never of the will itself, nor of the Idea in which it adequately objectifies itself. So then of every particular movement or change of any kind in nature, a cause is to be sought, that is, a condition that of necessity produced it, but never of the natural force itself which is revealed in this and innumerable similar phenomena; and it is therefore simple misunderstanding, arising from want of consideration, to ask for a cause of gravity, electricity, and so on. Only if one had somehow shown that gravity and electricity were not original special forces of Nature, but only the manifestations of a more general force already known, would it be allowable to ask for the cause which made this force produce the phenomena of gravity or of electricity here. All this has been explained at length above. In the same way every particular act of will of a knowing individual (which is itself only a manifestation of will as the thing-in-itself) has necessarily a motive without which that act would never have occurred; but just as material causes contain merely the determination that at this time, in this place, and in this matter, a manifestation of this or that natural force must take place, so the motive determines only the act of will of a knowing being, at this time, in this place, and under these circumstances, as a particular act, but by no means determines that that being wills in general or wills in this manner; this is the expression of his intelligible character, which, as will itself, the thing-in-itself, is without ground, for it lies outside the province of the principle of sufficient reason. Therefore every man has permanent aims and motives by which he guides his conduct, and he can always give an account of his particular actions; but if he were asked why he wills at all, or why in general he wills to exist, he would have no answer, and the question would indeed seem to him meaningless; and this would be just the expression of his consciousness that he himself is nothing but will, whose willing stands by itself and requires more particular determination by motives only in its individual acts at each point of time.

In fact, freedom from all aim, from all limits, belongs to the nature of the will, which is an endless striving. The plant raises its manifestation from the seed through the stem and the leaf to the blossom and the fruit, which again is the beginning of a new seed, a new individual, that runs through the old course, and so on through endless time. Such also is the life of the animal; procreation is its highest point, and after attaining to it, the life of the first individual quickly or slowly sinks, while a new life ensures to nature the endurance of the species and repeats the same phenomena. Indeed, the constant renewal of the matter of every organism is also to be regarded as merely the manifestation of this continual pressure and change, and physiologists are now ceasing to hold that it is the necessary reparation of the matter wasted in motion, for the possible wearing out of the machine can by no means be equivalent to the support it is constantly receiving through nourishment. Eternal becoming, endless flux, characterizes the revelation of the inner nature of will. Finally, the same things shows itself in human endeavours and desires, which always delude us by presenting their satisfaction as the final end of will. As soon as we attain to them they no longer appear the same, and therefore they soon grow stale, are forgotten, and though not openly disowned, are yet always thrown aside as vanished illusions. We are fortunate enough if there still remains something to wish for and to strive after, that the game may be kept up of constant transition from desires to satisfaction, and from satisfaction to a new desire, the rapid course of which is called happiness, and the slow course sorrow, and does not sink into that stagnation that shows itself in fearful ennui that paralyses life, vain yearning without a definite object, deadening languor. According to all this, when the will is enlightened by knowledge, it always knows what it wills now and here, never what it wills in general; every particular act of will has its end, the whole will has none; just as every particular phenomenon of Nature is determined by a sufficient cause so far as concerns its appearance in this place at this time, but the force which manifests itself in it has no general cause, for it belongs to the thing-in-itself, to the groundless will.

Third Book
The World as Idea

Second Aspect

THE IDEA INDEPENDENT OF THE PRINCIPLE OF SUFFICIENT
REASON: THE PLATONIC IDEA: THE OBJECT OF ART

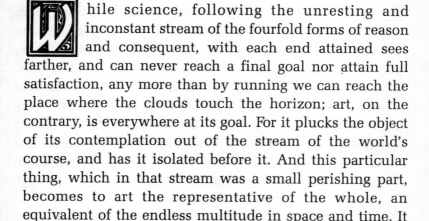hile science, following the unresting and inconstant stream of the fourfold forms of reason and consequent, with each end attained sees farther, and can never reach a final goal nor attain full satisfaction, any more than by running we can reach the place where the clouds touch the horizon; art, on the contrary, is everywhere at its goal. For it plucks the object of its contemplation out of the stream of the world's course, and has it isolated before it. And this particular thing, which in that stream was a small perishing part, becomes to art the representative of the whole, an equivalent of the endless multitude in space and time. It

therefore pauses at this particular thing; the course of time stops; the relations vanish for it; only the essential, the Idea, is its object. We may, therefore, accurately define it as the *way of viewing things independent of the principle of sufficient reason*, in opposition to the way of viewing them which proceeds in accordance with that principle, and which is the method of experience and of science. This last method of considering things may be compared to a line infinitely extended in a horizontal direction, and the former to a vertical line which cuts it at any point. The method of viewing things which proceeds in accordance with the principle of sufficient reason is the rational method, and it alone is valid and of use in practical life and in science. The method which looks away from the content of this principle is the method of genius, which is only valid and of use in art. The first is the method of Aristotle; the second is, on the whole, that of Plato. The first is like the mighty storm, that rushes along without beginning and without aim, bending, agitating, and carrying away everything before it; the second is like the silent sunbeam, that pierces through the storm quite unaffected by it. The first is like the innumerable showering drops of the waterfall, which, constantly changing, never rest for an instant; the second is like the rainbow, quietly resting on this raging torrent. Only through the pure contemplation described above, which ends entirely in the object, can Ideas be comprehended; and the nature of *genius* consists in pre-eminent capacity for such contemplation. Now, as this requires that a man should entirely forget himself, and the relations in which he stands, *genius* is simply the completest *objectivity, i.e.,* the objective tendency of the mind, as opposed to the subjective, which is directed to one's own self—in other words, to the will. Thus genius is the faculty of continuing in the state of pure perception, of losing oneself in perception, and of enlisting in this service the knowledge which originally existed only for the service of the will; that is to say, genius is the power of leaving one's own interests, wishes, and aims entirely out of sight, thus of entirely renouncing one's own personality for a time, so as to remain *pure knowing subject*, clear vision of the world; and this not merely at moments, but for a sufficient length of time, and with sufficient consciousness, to enable one to reproduce by deliberate art what has thus been apprehended, and "to fix in lasting thoughts the wavering images that float before the mind." It is as if, when genius appears in an individual, a far larger measure of the power of knowledge falls to his lot than is necessary for the service of an individual will; and this superfluity of knowledge, being free, now becomes subject purified from will, a clear mirror of the inner nature of the world.

The common mortal, that manufacture of Nature which she produces by the thousand every day, is as we have said, not capable, at least not continuously so, of observation that in every sense is wholly disinterested, as sensuous contemplation, strictly so called, is. He can turn his attention to things only so far as they have some relation to his will, however indirect it may be. Since in this respect, which never demands anything but the knowledge of relations, the abstract conception of the thing is sufficient, and for the most part even better adapted for use; the ordinary man does not linger long over the mere perception, does not fix his attention long on one object, but in all that is presented to him hastily seeks merely the concept under which it is to be brought, as the lazy man seeks a chair, and then it interests him no further. The man of genius, on the other hand, whose excessive power of knowledge frees it at times from the service of will, dwells on the consideration of life itself, strives to comprehend the Idea of each thing, not its relations to other things; and in doing this he often forgets to consider his own path in life, and therefore for the most part pursues its awkwardly enough. While to the ordinary man his faculty of knowledge is a lamp to lighten his path, to the man of genius it is the sun which reveals the world. This great diversity in their way of looking at life soon becomes visible in the outward appearance both of the man of genius and of the ordinary mortal. The man in whom genius lives and works is easily distinguished by his glance, which is both keen and steady, and bears the stamp of perception, of contemplation. This is easily seen from the likenesses of the few men of genius whom Nature has produced here and there among countless millions. On the other hand, in the case of an ordinary man, the true object of his contemplation, what he is prying into, can be easily seen from his glance, if indeed it is not quite stupid and vacant, as is generally the case. Therefore the expression of genius in a face consists in this, that in it a decided predominance of knowledge over will is visible, and consequently there also shows itself in it a knowledge that is entirely devoid of relation to will, *i.e., pure knowing*.

On the contrary, in ordinary countenances there is a predominant expression of will; and we see that knowledge only comes into activity under the impulse of will, and thus is directed merely by motives.

It has often been remarked that there is a side at which genius and madness touch, and even pass over into each other, and indeed poetical inspiration has been called a kind of madness: *amabilis insania,* Horace calls it (*Od.* iii. 4), and Wieland in the introduction to *Oberon* speaks of it as "amiable madness." Even Aristotle, as quoted by Seneca (*De Tranq. Animi,* 15, 16), is reported to have said: *Nullum magnum ingenium sine mixture dementiæ fuit.* Plato expresses it in the figure of the dark cave, referred to above (*De Rep.* 7), when he says: "Those who, outside the cave, have seen the true sunlight and the things that have true being (Ideas), cannot afterwards see properly down in the cave, because their eyes are not accustomed to the darkness; they cannot distinguish the shadows, and are jeered at for their mistakes by those who have never left the cave and its shadows." In the *Phædrus* also (p. 317), he distinctly says that there can be no true poet without a certain madness; in fact (p. 327), that everyone appears mad who recognizes the eternal Ideas in fleeting things. Cicero also quotes: *Negat enim sine furore, Democritus, quemquam poetam magnum esse posse; quod idem dicit Plato* (*De Devin.,* i. 37). And lastly, Pope says:

"Great wits to madness sure are near allied,
And thin partitions do their bounds divide."

❖

All *willing* arises from want, therefore from deficiency, and therefore from suffering. The satisfaction of a wish ends it; yet for one wish that is satisfied there remain at least ten which are denied. Further, the desire lasts long, the demands are infinite; the satisfaction is short and scantily measured out. But even the final satisfaction is itself only apparent; every satisfied wish at once makes room for a new one; both are illusions; the one is known to be so, the other not yet. No attained object of desire can give lasting satisfaction, but merely a fleeting gratification; it is like the alms thrown to the beggar, that keeps him alive today that his misery may be prolonged till the morrow. Therefore, so long as our consciousness is filled by our will, so long as we are given up to the throng of desires with their constant hopes and fears, so long as we are the subject of willing, we can never have lasting happiness nor peace. It is essentially all the same whether we pursue or flee, fear injury or seek enjoyment; the care for the constant demands of the will, in whatever form it may be, continually occupies and sways the consciousness; but without peace no true well-being is possible. The subject of willing is thus constantly stretched on the revolving wheels of Ixion, pours water into the sieve of the Danaids, is the ever-longing Tantalis.

But when some external cause or inward disposition lifts us suddenly out of the endless stream of willing, delivers knowledge from the slavery of the will, the attention is no longer directed to the motives of willing, but comprehends things free from their relation to the will, and thus observes them without personal interest, without subjectivity, purely objectively, gives itself entirely up to them so far as they are ideas, but not in so far as they are motives. Then all at once the peace which we were always seeking, but which always fled from us on the former path of the desires, comes to us of its own accord, and it is well with us. It is the painless state which Epicurus prizes as the highest good and as the state of the gods; for we are for the moment set free from the miserable striving of the will; we keep the Sabbath of the penal servitude of willing; the wheel of Ixion stands still.

But this is just the state which I described above as necessary for the knowledge of the Idea, as pure contemplation, as sinking oneself in perception, losing oneself in the object, forgetting all individuality, surrendering that kind of knowledge which follows the principle of sufficient reason, and comprehends only relations; the state by means of which at once and inseparably the perceived particular thing is raised to the Idea of its whole species, and the knowing individual to the pure subject of will-less knowledge, and as such they are both taken out of the stream of time and all other relations. It is then all one whether we see the sun set from the prison or from the palace.

Lastly, it is this blessedness of will-less perception which casts an enchanting glamour over the past and distant, and presents them to us in so fair a light by means of self-deception. For as we think of days long gone by, days in which we lived in a distant place, it is only the objects which our fancy recalls, not the subject of will, which bore about with it then its incurable sorrows, just as it bears them now; but they are forgotten, because since then they have often given place to others. Now, objective perception acts with regard to what is remembered just as it would in what is present, if we let it have influence over us, if we surrendered ourselves to it free from will. Hence it arises that, especially when we are more than ordinarily disturbed by some want, the remembrance of past and distant scenes suddenly flits across our minds like a lost paradise. The fancy recalls only what was objective, not what was individually subjective, and we imagine that that objective stood before us then just as pure and undisturbed by any relation to the will as its image stands in our fancy now; while in reality the relation of the objects to our will gave us pain then just as it does now. We can deliver ourselves from all suffering just as well through present objects as through distant ones whenever we raise ourselves to a purely objective contemplation of them, and so are able to bring about the illusion that only the objects are present and not we ourselves. Then, as the pure subject of knowledge, freed from the miserable self, we become entirely one with these objects, and, for the moment, our wants are as foreign to us as they are to them. The world as idea alone remains, and the world as will has disappeared.

Human beauty is an objective expression, which means the fullest objectification of will at the highest grade at which it is knowable, the Idea of man in general, completely expressed in the sensible form. But however much the objective side of the beautiful appears here the subjective side still always accompanies it. And just because no object transports us so quickly into pure æsthetic contemplation, as the most beautiful human countenance and form, at the sight of which we are instantly filled with unspeakable satisfaction, and raised above ourselves and all that troubles us; this is only possible because this most distinct and purest knowledge of will raises us most easily and quickly to the state of pure knowing, in which our personality, our will with its constant pain, disappears, so long as the pure æsthetic pleasure lasts. Therefore it is that Goethe says: "No evil can touch him who looks on human beauty; he feels himself at one with himself and with the world." That a beautiful human form is produced by nature must be explained in this way. At this its highest grade the will objectifies itself in an individual; and therefore through circumstances and its own power it completely overcomes all the hindrances and opposition which the phenomena of the lower grades present to it. Such are the forces of Nature, from which the will must always first extort and win back the matter that belongs to all its manifestations. Further, the phenomenon of will at its highest grades always has multiplicity in its form. Even the tree is only a systematic aggregate of innumerably repeated sprouting fibres. This combination assumes greater complexity in higher forms, and the human body is an exceedingly complex system of different parts, each of which has a peculiar life of its own, *vita propria*, subordinate to the whole. Now that all these parts are in the proper fashion subordinate to the whole,

and co-ordinate to each other, that they all work together
harmoniously for the expression of the whole, nothing
superfluous, nothing restricted; all these are the rare
conditions, whose result is beauty, the completely
expressed character of the species. So is it in Nature. But
how in art? One would suppose that art achieved the
beautiful by imitating nature. But how is the artist to
recognize the perfect work which is to be imitated, and
distinguish it from the failures, if he does not anticipate
the beautiful *before experience*? And besides this, has
nature ever produced a human being perfectly beautiful
in all his parts? That we all recognize human beauty when
we see it, but that in the true artist this takes place with
such clearness that he shows it as he has never seen it,
and surpasses nature in his representation; this is only
possible because *we ourselves* are the will whose adequate
objectification at its highest grade is here to be judged and
discovered. Thus alone have we in fact an anticipation of
that which nature (which is just the will that constitutes
our own being) strives to express. And in the true genius
this anticipation is accompanied by so great a degree of
intelligence that he recognizes the Idea in the particular
thing, and thus, as it were, *understands the half-uttered
speech of nature*, and articulates clearly what she only
stammered forth. He expresses in the hard marble that
beauty of form which in a thousand attempts she failed
to produce, he presents it to nature, saying, as it were, to
her, "That is what you wanted to say!" And whoever is able
to judge replies, "Yes, that is it."

It is true that both experience and history teach us to

know man; yet oftener men than man, *i.e.*, they give us empirical notes of the behaviour of men to each other, from which we may frame rules for our own conduct, oftener than they afford us deep glimpses of the inner nature of man. The latter function, however, is by no means entirely denied them; but as often as it is the nature of mankind itself that discloses itself to us in history or in our own experience, we have comprehended our experience, and the historian has comprehended history, with artistic eyes, poetically, *i.e.*, according to the Idea, not the phenomenon, in its indispensable condition of understanding poetry as of understanding history; for it is, so to speak, the dictionary of the language that both speak. But history is related to poetry as portrait-painting is related to historical painting; the one gives us the true in the individual, the other the true in the universal; the one has the truth of the phenomenon, and can therefore verify it from the phenomenal, the other has the truth of the Idea, which can be found in no particular phenomenon, but yet speaks to us from them all. The poet from deliberate choice represents significant characters in significant situations; the historian takes both as they come. Indeed, he must regard and select the circumstances and the persons, not with reference to their inward and true significance, which expresses the Idea, but according to the outward, apparent and relatively important significance with regard to the connection and the consequences. He must consider nothing in and for itself in its essential character and expression, but must look at everything in its relations, in its connection, in its influence upon what follows, and especially upon its own age. Therefore he will not overlook an action of a king, though of little significance, and in itself quite common, because it has results and influence. And, on the other hand, actions of the highest significance of particular and very eminent individuals are not to be recorded by him if they have no consequences. For his treatment follows the principle of sufficient reason, and apprehends the phenomenon, of which this principle is the form. But the poet comprehends the Idea, the inner nature of man apart from all relations, outside all time, the adequate objectivity of the thing-in-itself, at its highest grade. Therefore, whoever desires to know man in his inner nature, identical in all its phenomena and developments, to know him according to the Idea, will find that the works of the great, immortal poet present a far truer, more distinct picture, than the historians can ever give. For even the best of the historians are, as poets, far from the first; and moreover their hands are tied.

Tragedy is to be regarded, and is recognized as the summit of poetical art, both on account of the greatness of its effect and the difficulty of its achievement. It is very significant for our whole system, and well worthy of observation, that the end of this highest poetical achievement is the representation of the terrible side of life. The unspeakable pain, the wail of humanity, the triumph of evil, the scornful mastery of chance, and the irretrievable fall of the just and innocent is here presented to us; and in this lies a significant hint of the nature of the world and of existence. It is the strife of will with itself, which here, completely unfolded at the highest grade of its objectivity, comes into fearful prominence. It becomes visible in the suffering of men, which is now introduced, partly through chance and error, which appear as the rulers of the world, personified as fate, on account of their insidiousness, which even reaches the appearance of design; partly it proceeds from man himself, through the self-mortifying efforts of a few, through the wickedness and perversity of most. It is one and the same will that lives and appears in them all, but whose phenomena fight against each other and destroy each other. In one individual it appears powerfully, in another more weakly; in one more subject to reason, and softened by the light of knowledge, in another less so, till at last, in some single case, this knowledge, purified and heightened by suffering itself, reaches the point at which the phenomenon, the veil of Maya, no longer deceives it. It sees through the form of the phenomenon, the *principium individuationis*. The egoism which rests on this perishes with it, so that now the *motives* that were so powerful before have lost their might, and instead of them the complete knowledge of the nature of the world, which has a *quieting* effect on the will, produces resignation, the surrender not merely of life, but of the very will to live. Thus we see in tragedies the noblest men, after long conflict and suffering, at last renounce the ends they have so keenly followed, and all the pleasures of life for ever, or else freely and joyfully surrender life itself. So is it with the steadfast prince of Calderon; with Gretchen in *Faust*; with Hamlet, whom his friend Horatio would willingly follow, but is bade remain a while, and in this harsh world draw his breath in pain, to tell the story of Hamlet, and clear his memory; so also is it with the Maid of Orleans, the Bride of Messina; they all die purified by suffering, *i.e.*, after the will to live which was formerly in them is dead. In the *Mohammed* of Voltaire this is actually expressed in the concluding words which the dying Palmira addresses to Mohammed: "The world is for tyrants: live!" On the other hand, the demand for so-called poetical justice rests on entire misconception of the nature of tragedy, and, indeed, of the nature of the world itself. It boldly appears in all its dullness in the criticisms which Dr. Samuel Johnson made on particular plays of Shakespeare, for he very naïvely laments its entire absence. And its absence is certainly obvious, for in what has Ophelia, Desdemona, or Cordelia offended? But only the dull, optimistic, Protestant-rationalistic or peculiarly Jewsih view of life will make the demand for poetical justice, and find satisfaction in it. The true sense of tragedy is the deeper insight, that it is not his own individual sins that the hero atones for, but original sin, *i.e.*, the crime of existence itself:

> "Pues el delito mayor
> Del hombre es haber nacido;"

> ("For the greatest crime of man
> Is that he was born;")

as Calderon exactly expresses it.

I gave my mind entirely up to the impression of music in all its forms, and then returned to reflection and the system of thought expressed in the present work, and thus I arrived at an explanation of the inner nature of music and of the nature of its imitative relation of the world—which from analogy had necessarily to be pre-supposed—an explanation which is quite sufficient for myself, and satisfactory to my investigation, and which will doubtless be equally evident to anyone who has followed me thus far and has agreed with my view of the world. Yet I recognize the fact that it is essentially impossible to prove this explanation, for it assumes and establishes a relation of music, as idea, to that which from its nature can never be idea, and music will have to be regarded as the copy of an original which can never itself be directly presented as idea. I can therefore do no more than state here, at the conclusion of this Third Book, which has been principally devoted to the consideration of the arts, the explanation of the marvellous art of music which satisfies myself, and I must leave the acceptance or denial of my view to the effect produced upon each of my readers both by music itself and by the whole system of thought communicated in this work. Moreover, I regard it as necessary, in order to be able to assent with full conviction to the exposition of the significance of music I am about to give, that one should often listen to music with constant reflection upon my theory concerning it, and for this again it is necessary to be very familiar with the whole of my system of thought.

The (Platonic) Ideas are the adequate objectification of will. To excite or suggest the knowledge of these by means of the representation of particular things (for works of art themselves are always representations of particular things) is the end of all the other arts, which can only be attained by a corresponding change in the knowing subject. Thus all these arts objectify the will directly only by means of the Ideas; and since our world is nothing but the manifestation of the Ideas in multiplicity, though their entrance into the *principium individuationis* (the form of the knowledge possible for the individual as such), music also, since it passes over the Ideas, is entirely independent of the phenomenal world, ignores it altogether, could to a certain extent exist if there was no world at all, which cannot be said of the other arts. Music is as *direct* an objectification and copy of the whole *will* as the world itself, nay, even as the Ideas, whose multiplied manifestation constitutes the world of individual things. Music is thus by no means like the other arts, the copy of the Ideas, but the *copy of the will itself,* whose objectivity the Ideas are. This is why the effect of music is so much more powerful and penetrating than that of the other arts, for they speak only of shadows, but it speaks of the thing itself. Since, however, it is the same will which objectifies itself both in the Ideas and in music, though in quite different ways, there must be, not indeed a direct likeness, but yet a parallel, an analogy, between music and the Ideas whose manifestation in multiplicity and incompleteness is the visible world.

Now the nature of man consists in this, that his will strives, is satisfied and strives anew, and so on for ever. Indeed, his happiness and well-being consist simply in the quick transition from wish to satisfaction, and from satisfaction to a new wish. For the absence of satisfaction is suffering, the empty longing for a new wish, languor, *ennui*. And corresponding to this the nature of melody is a constant digression and deviation from the keynote in a thousand ways, not only to the harmonious intervals to the third and dominant, but to every tone, to the dissonant sevenths and to the superfluous degrees; yet there always follows a constant return to the key-note. In all these deviations melody expresses the multifarious efforts of will, but always its satisfaction also by the final return to an harmonious interval, and still more, to the key-note. The composition of melody, the disclosure in it of all the deepest secrets of human willing and feeling, is the work of genius, whose action, which is more apparent here than anywhere else, lies far from all reflection and conscious intention, and may be called an inspiration. The conception is here, as everywhere in art, unfruitful. The composer reveals the inner nature of the world, and expresses the deepest wisdom in a language which his reason does not understand; as a person under the influence of mesmerism tells things of which he has no conception when he awakes. Therefore in the composer, more than in any other artist, the man is entirely separated and distinct from the artist.

According to all this, we may regard the phenomenal world, or Nature, and music as two different expressions of the same thing, which is therefore itself the only medium of their analogy, so that a knowledge of it is demanded in order to understand that analogy. Music, therefore, if regarded as an expression of the world, is in the highest degree a universal language, which is related indeed to the universality of concepts, much as they are related to the particular things. Its universality, however, is by no means that empty universality of abstraction, but quite of a different kind, and is united with thorough and distinct definiteness. In this respect it resembles geometrical figures and numbers, which are the universal forms of all possible objects of experience and applicable to them all *a priori*, and yet are not abstract but perceptible and thoroughly determined. The unutterable depth of all music by virtue of which it floats through our consciousness as the vision of a paradise firmly believed in yet ever distant from us, and by which also it is so fully understood and yet so inexplicable, rests on the fact that it restores to us all the emotions of our inmost nature, but entirely without reality and far removed from their pain. So also the seriousness which is essential to it, which excludes the absurd from its direct and peculiar province, is to be explained by the fact that its object is not the idea, with reference to which alone deception and absurdity are possible; but its object is directly the will, and this is essentially the most serious of all things, for it is that on which all depends.

I might still have something to say about the way in which music is perceived, namely, in and through time alone, with absolute exclusion of space, and also apart from the influence of the knowledge of causality, thus without understanding; for the tones make the æsthetic impression as effect, and without obliging us to go back to their causes, as in the case of perception. I do not wish, however, to lengthen this discussion, as I have perhaps already gone too much into detail with regard to some things in this Third Book, or have dwelt too much on particulars. But my aim made it necessary, and it will be the less disapproved if the importance and high worth of art, which is seldom sufficiently recognized, be kept in mind. For if, according to our view, the whole visible world is just the objectification, the mirror, of the will, conducting it to knowledge of itself, and, indeed, as we shall soon see, to the possibility of its deliverance; and if, at the same time, the world as idea, if we regard it in isolation, and, freeing ourselves from all volition, allow it alone to take possession of our consciousness, is the most joy-giving and the only innocent side of life; we must regard art as the higher ascent, the more complete development of all this, for it achieves essentially just what is achieved by the visible world itself, only with greater concentration, more perfectly, with intention and intelligence, and therefore may be called, in the full significance of the word, the flower of life. If the whole world as idea is only the visibility of will, the work of art is to render this visibility more distinct. It is the *camera obscura* which shows the objects more purely, and enables us to survey them and comprehend them better. It is the play within the play, the stage upon the stage in *Hamlet.*

The pleasure we receive from all beauty, the consolation which art affords, the enthusiasm of the artist—which enables him to forget the cares of life—the latter an advantage of the man of genius over other men, which alone repays him for the suffering that increases in proportion to the clearness of consciousness, and for the desert loneliness among men of a different race—all this rests on the fact that the in-itself of life, the will, existence itself, is, as we shall see farther on, a constant sorrow, partly miserable, partly terrible; while, on the contrary, as idea alone, purely contemplated, or copied by art, free from pain, it presents to us a drama full of significance. This purely knowable side of the world, and the copy of it in any art, is the element of the artist. He is chained to the contemplation of the play, the objectification of will; he remains beside it, does not get tired of contemplating it and representing it in copies; and meanwhile he bears himself the cost of the production of that play, *i.e.*, he himself is the will which objectifies itself, and remains in constant suffering. That pure, true and deep knowledge of the inner nature of the world becomes now for him an end in itself: he stops there. Therefore it does not become to him a quieter of the will, as, we shall see in the next book, it does in the case of the saint who has attained to resignation; it does not deliver him for ever from life, but only at moments, and is therefore not for him a path out of life, but only an occasional consolation in it, till his power, increased by this contemplation and at last tired of the play, lays hold on the real. The St. Cecilia of Raphael may be regarded as a representation of this transition. To the real, then, we now turn in the following book.

❖

Fourth Book
The World as Will

Second Aspect

THE ASSERTION AND DENIAL OF THE WILL TO LIVE, WHEN
SELF-CONSCIOUSNESS HAS BEEN ATTAINED

Will is the thing-in-itself, the inner content, the essence of the world. Life, the visible world, the phenomenon, is only the mirror of the will. Therefore life accompanies the will as inseparably as the shadow accompanies the body; and if will exists, so will life, the world, exist. Life is, therefore, assured to the will to live; and so long as we are filled with the will to live we need have no fear for our existence, even in the presence of death. It is true we see the individual come into being and pass away; but the individual is only phenomenal, exists only for the knowledge which is bound to the principle of sufficient reason, to the *principium individuationis.* Certainly, for this kind of knowledge, the individual receives his life as a gift, rises out of nothing, then suffers the loss of this gift through death, and returns again to nothing. But we desire to consider life philosophically, *i.e.,* according to its Ideas, and in this sphere we shall find that neither the will, the thing-in-itself in all phenomena, nor the subject of knowing, that which perceives all phenomena, is affected at all by birth or by death. Birth and death belong merely of the phenomenon of will, thus to life; and it is essential to this to exhibit itself in individuals which come into being and pass away, as fleeting phenomena appearing in the form of time—phenomena of that which in itself knows no time, but must exhibit itself precisely in the way we have said, in order to objectify its peculiar nature. Birth and death belong in like manner to life, and hold the balance as reciprocal conditions of each other, or, if one likes the expression, as poles of the whole phenomenon of life. The wisest of all mythologies, the Indian, expresses this by giving to the very god that symbolizes destruction, death (as Brahma, the most sinful and the lowest god of the Trimurti symbolizes generation, coming into being, and Vishnu maintaining or preserving), by giving, I say, to Siva as an attribute not only the necklace of skulls, but also the lingam, the symbol of generation, which appears here as the counterpart of death, thus signifying that generation and death are essentially correlatives, which reciprocally neutralize and annul each other. It was precisely the same sentiment that led the Greeks and Romans to adorn their costly sarcophagi, just as we see them now, with feasts, dances, marriages, the chase, fights of wild beasts, bacchanalians, etc.; thus with representations of the full ardour of life, which they place before us not only in such revels and sports, but also in sensual groups, and even go so far as to represent the sexual intercourse of satyrs and goats. Clearly the aim was to point in the most impressive manner away from the death of the mourned individual to the immortal life of nature, and thus to indicate, though without abstract knowledge, that the whole of nature is the phenomenon and also the fulfilment of the will to live. The form of this phenomenon is time, space and causality, and by means of these individuation, which carries with it that the individual must come into being and pass away. But this no more affects the will to live, of whose manifestation the individual is, as it were, only a particular example or specimen, than the death of an individual injures the whole of Nature. For it is not the individual, but only the species that Nature cares for, and for the preservation of which she so earnestly strives, providing for it with the utmost prodigality through the vast surplus of the seed and the great strength of the fructifying impulse. The individual, on the contrary, neither has nor can have any value for Nature, for her kingdom is infinite time and infinite space, and in these infinite multiplicity of possible individuals. Therefore she is always ready to let the individual fall, and hence it is not only exposed to destruction in a thousand ways by the most insignificant accident, but originally destined for it, and conducted towards it by Nature herself from the moment it has served its end of maintaining the species. Thus Nature naïvely expresses the great truth that only the Ideas, not the individuals, have, properly speaking, reality, *i.e.*, are complete objectivity of the will. Now, since man is Nature itself, and indeed Nature at the highest grade of its self-consciousness, but Nature is only the objectified will to live, the man who has comprehended and retained this point of view may well console himself, when contemplating his own death and that of his friends, by turning his eyes to the immortal life of Nature, which he himself is. This is the significance of Siva with the lingam, and of those ancient sarcophagi with their pictures of glowing life, which say to the mourning beholder, *Natura non contristatur.*

Above all things, we must distinctly recognize that the form of the phenomenon of will, the form of life or reality, is really only the *present*, not the future nor the past. The latter are only in the conception, exist only in the connection of knowledge, so far as it follows the principle of sufficient reason. No man has ever lived in the past, and none will live in the future; the *present* alone is the form of all life, and is its sure possession which can never be taken from it. The present always exists, together with its content. Both remain fixed without wavering, like the rainbow on the waterfall. For life is firm and certain in the will, and the present is firm and certain in life. Certainly, if we reflect on the thousands of years that are past, of the millions of men who lived in them, we ask, What were they? What has become of them? But, on the other hand, we need only recall our own past life and renew its scenes vividly in our imagination, and then ask again, What was all this? What has become of it? As it is with it, so is it with the life of those millions. Or should we suppose that the past could receive a new existence because it has been sealed by death? Our own past, the most recent part of it, and even yesterday, is now no more than an empty dream of the fancy, and such is the past of all those millions. What was? What is? The will, of which of life is the mirror, and knowledge free from will, which beholds it clearly in that mirror. Whoever has not yet recognized this, or will not recognize it, must add to the question asked above as to the fate of past generations of men this question also: Why he, the questioner, is so fortunate as to be conscious of this costly, fleeting and only real present, while those hundreds of generations of men, even the heroes and philosophers of those ages, have sunk into the night of the past, and have thus become nothing; but he, his insignificant ego, actually exists? Or more shortly, though somewhat strangely: Why this now, his now, *is* just now and *was* not long ago? Since he asks such strange questions, he regards his existence and his time as independent of each other, and the former as projected into the latter. He assumes indeed two nows—one which belongs to the object, the other which belongs to the subject, and marvels at the happy accident of their coincidence. But in truth, only the point of contact of the object, the form of which is time, with the subject, which has no mode of the principle of sufficient reason as its form, constitutes the present, as is shown in the essay on the principle of sufficient reason. Now all object is the will so far as it has become idea, and the subject is the necessary correlative of the object. But real objects are only in the present; the past and the future contain only conceptions and fancies, therefore the present is the essential form of the phenomenon of the will, and inseparable from it. The present alone is that which always exists and remains immovable. That which, empirically apprehended, is the most transitory of all, presents itself to the metaphysical vision, which sees beyond the forms of empirical perception, as that which alone endures, the *nunc stans* of the schoolmen. The source and the supporter of its content is the will to live or the thing-in-itself—which we are. That which constantly becomes and passes away, in that it has either already been or is still to be, belongs to the phenomenon as such on account of its forms, which make coming into being and passing away possible. Accordingly, we must think: *Quid fuit?—Quod est. Quid erit?—Quod fuit*; and take it in the strict meaning of the words; thus understand not *simile* but *idem*. For life is certain to the will, and the present is certain to life. Thus it is that everyone can say, "I am once for all lord of the present, and through all eternity it will accompany me as my shadow: therefore I do not wonder where it has come from, and how it happens that it is exactly now." Time is like an unceasing stream, and the present a rock on which the stream breaks itself, but does not carry away with it. The will, as thing-in-itself, is just as little subordinate to the principle of sufficient reason as the subject of knowledge, which, finally, in a certain regard is the will itself or its expression. And as life, its own phenomenon, is assured to the will, so is the present, the single form of real life. Therefore we have not to investigate the past before life, not the future after death: we have rather to know the *present*, the one form in which the will manifests itself. It will not escape from the will, but neither will the will escape from it. If, therefore, life as it is satisfies, whoever affirms it in every way may regard it with confidence as endless, and banish the fear of death as an illusion that inspires him with the foolish dread that he can ever be robbed of the present, and foreshadows a time in which there is no present; an illusion with regard to time analogous to the illusion with regard to space through which everyone imagines the position on the globe he happens to occupy as above, and all other places as below. In the same way everyone links the present to his own individuality, and imagines that all present is extinguished with it; that then past and future might be without a present. But as on the surface of the globe every place is above, so the form of all life is the *present*, and to fear death because it robs us of the present, is just as foolish as to fear that we may slip down from the round globe upon which we have now the good fortune to occupy the upper surface. The present is the form essential to the objectification of the will. It cuts time, which extends infinitely in both directions, as a mathematical point, and stands immovably fixed, like an everlasting midday with no cool evening, as the actual sun burns without intermission, while it only seems to sink into the bosom of night. Therefore if a man fears death as his annihilation, it is just as if he were to think that the sun cries out at evening, "Woe is me! for I go down into eternal night." And conversely, whoever is oppressed with the burden of life, whoever desires life and affirms it, but abhors its torments, and especially can no longer endure the hard lot that has fallen to himself, such a man has no deliverance to hope for from death, and cannot right himself by suicide. The cool shades of Orcus allure him only with the false appearance of a haven of rest. The earth rolls from day into night, the individual dies, but the sun itself shines without intermission, an eternal noon. Life is assured to the will to life; the form of life is an endless present, no matter how the individuals, the phenomena of the Idea, arise and pass away in time, like fleeting dreams.

Dogmas change and our knowledge is deceptive; but Nature never errs, her procedure is sure, and the never conceals it. Everything is entirely in Nature and Nature is entire in everything. She has her centre in every brute. It has surely found its way into existence, and it will surely find its way out of it. In the meantime it lives, fearless and without care, in the presence of annihilation, supported by the consciousness that it is nature herself, and imperishable as she is. Man alone carries about with him, in abstract conceptions, the certainty of his death; yet this can only trouble him very rarely, when for a single moment some occasion calls it up to his imagination. Against the mighty voice of Nature reflection can do little. In man, as in the brute which does not think, the certainty that springs from his inmost consciousness that he himself is Nature, the world, predominates as a lasting frame of mind; and on account of this no man is observably disturbed by the thought of certain and never-distant death, but lives as if he would live for ever. Indeed this is carried so far that we may say that no one has really a lively conviction of the certainty of his death, otherwise there would be no great difference between his frame of mind and that of a condemned criminal. Everyone recognizes that certainty in the abstract and theoretically, but lays it aside like other theoretical truths which are not applicable to practice, without really receiving it into his living consciousness.

At every grade that is enlightened by knowledge, the will appears as an individual. The human individual finds himself as finite in infinite space and time, and consequently as a vanishing quantity compared with them. He is projected into them, and, on account of their unlimited nature, he has always a merely relative, never absolute *when* and *where* of his existence; for his place and duration are finite parts of what is infinite and boundless. His real existence is only in the present, whose unchecked flight into the past is a constant transition into death, a constant dying. For his past life, apart from its possible consequences for the present, and the testimony regarding the will that is expressed in it, is now entirely done with, dead and no longer anything; and, therefore, it must be, as a matter of reason, indifferent to him whether the content of that past was pain or pleasure. But the present is always passing through his hands into the past; the future is quite uncertain and always short. Thus his existence, even when we consider only its formal side, is a constant hurrying of the present into the dead past, a constant dying. But if we look at it from the physical side, it is clear that, as our walking is admittedly merely a constantly prevented falling, the life of our body is only a constantly prevented dying, an ever-postponed death: finally, in the same way, the activity of our mind is a constantly deferred ennui. Every breath we draw wards off the death that is constantly intruding upon us. In this way we fight with it every moment, and again, at longer intervals, through every meal we eat, every sleep we take, every time we warm ourselves, etc. In the end, death must conquer, for we became subject to him through birth, and he only plays for a little while with his prey before he swallows it up. We pursue our life, however, with great interest and much solicitude as long as possible, as we blow out a soap-bubble as long and as large as possible, although we know perfectly well that it will burst.

We saw that the inner being of unconscious nature is a constant striving without end and without rest. And this appears to us much more distinctly when we consider the nature of brutes and man. Willing and striving is its whole being, which may be very well compared to an unquenchable thirst. But the basis of all willing is need, deficiency and thus pain. Consequently, the nature of brutes and man is subject to pain originally and through its very being. If, on the other hand, it lacks objects of desire, because it is at once deprived of them by a too easy satisfaction, a terrible void and ennui comes over it, *i.e.*, its being and existence itself becomes an unbearable burden to it. Thus its life swings like a pendulum backwards and forwards between pain and ennui. This has also had to express itself very oddly in this way; after man had transferred all pain and torments to hell, there then remained nothing over for heaven but ennui.

Thus, between desiring and attaining, all human life flows on throughout. The wish is, in its nature, pain; the attainment soon begets satiety: the end was only apparent; possession takes away the charm; the wish, the need, presents itself under a new form; when it does not, then follows desolateness, emptiness, ennui, against which the conflict is just as painful as against want.

All satisfaction, or what is commonly called happiness, is always really and essentially only *negative*, and never positive. It is not an original gratification coming to us of itself, but must always be the satisfaction of a wish. The wish, *i.e.*, some want, is the condition which precedes every pleasure. But with the satisfaction the wish and therefore the pleasure cease. Thus the satisfaction of the pleasing can never be more than the deliverance from a pain, from a want; for such is not only every actual, open sorrow, but every desire, the importunity of which disturbs our peace, and, indeed, the deadening ennui also that makes life a burden to us. It is, however, so hard to attain or achieve anything; difficulties and troubles without end are opposed to every purpose, and at every step hindrances accumulate. But when finally everything is overcome and attained, nothing can ever be gained but deliverance from some sorrow or desire, so that we find ourselves just in the same position as we occupied before this sorrow or desire appeared. All that is even directly given us is merely the want, *i.e.*, the pain. The satisfaction and the pleasure

we can only know indirectly through the remembrance of
the preceding suffering and want, which ceases with its
appearance. Hence it arises that we are not properly conscious of the blessings and advantages we actually possess,
nor do we prize them, but think of them merely as a matter
of course, for they gratify us only negatively by restraining
suffering. Only when we have lost them do we become
sensible of their value; for the want, the privation, the
sorrow, is the positive, communicating itself directly to us.
Thus also we are pleased by the remembrance of past need,
sickness, want and such-like, because this is the only
means of enjoying the present blessings. And, further, it
cannot be denied that in this respect, and from this standpoint of egoism, which is the form of the will to live, the
sight or the description of the sufferings of others affords
us satisfaction and pleasure in precisely the way Lucretius
beautifully and frankly expresses it in the beginning of the
Second Book:

> "*Suave, mari magno, turbantibus æquora ventis,*
> *E terra Magnum alterius spectare laborem:*
> *Non, quia vexari quemquam est jucunda voluptas;*
> *Sed, quibus ipse malis careas, quia cernere suave est.*"

Everyone who has awakened from the first dream of youth,
who has considered his own experience and that of others,
who has studied himself in life, in the history of the past
and of his own time, and finally in the works of the great
poets, will, if his judgment is not paralysed by some

indelibly imprinted prejudice, certainly arrive at the conclusion that this human world is the kingdom of chance and error, which rule without mercy in great things and in small, and along with which folly and wickedness also wield the scourge. Hence it arises that everything better only struggles through with difficulty; what is noble and wise seldom attains to expression, becomes effective and claims attention, but the absurd and the perverse in the sphere of thought, the dull and tasteless in the sphere of art, the wicked and deceitful in the sphere of action, really assert a supremacy, only disturbed by short interruptions. On the other hand, everything that is excellent is always a mere exception, one case in millions, and therefore, if it presents itself in a lasting work, this, when it has outlived the enmity of its contemporaries, exists in isolation, is preserved like a meteoric stone, sprung from an order of things different from that which prevails here. But as far as the life of the individual is concerned, every biography is the history of suffering, for every life is, as a rule, a continual series of great and small misfortunes, which each one conceals as much as possible, because he knows that others can seldom feel sympathy or compassion, but almost always satisfaction at the sight of the woes from which they are themselves for the moment exempt. But perhaps at the end of life, if a man is sincere and in full possession of his faculties, he will never wish to have it to live over again, but rather than this, he will much prefer absolute annihilation. If, finally, we should bring clearly to a man's sight the terrible sufferings and miseries to which his life is constantly exposed, he would be seized with horror; and if we were to conduct the confirmed optimist through the hospitals, infirmaries and surgical operating-rooms, through the prisons, torture-chambers and slave-kennels, over battle-fields and places of execution; if we were to open to him all the dark abodes of misery, where it hides itself from the glance of cold curiosity, and, finally, allow him to glance into the starving dungeon of Ugolino, he, too, would understand at last the nature of this "best of possible worlds." For where did Dante take the materials for his hell but from this our actual world? And yet he made a very proper hell of it. And when, on the other hand, he came to the task of describing heaven and its delights, he had an insurmountable difficulty before him, for our world affords no materials at all for this. For the rest, I cannot here avoid the statement that, to me, *optimism*, when it is not merely the thoughtless talk of such as harbour nothing but words under their low foreheads, appears not merely as an absurd, but also as a really *wicked* way of thinking, as a bitter mockery of the unspeakable suffering of humanity. Let no one think that Christianity is favourable to optimism; for, on the contrary, in the Gospels world and evil are used as almost synonymous.

The maintenance of the body through its own powers is so small a degree of the assertion of will, that if it voluntarily remains at this degree, we might assume that, with the death of this body, the will also which appeared in it would be extinguished. But even the satisfaction of the sexual passions goes beyond the assertion of one's own existence, which fills so short a time, and asserts life for an indefinite time after the death of the individual. Nature, always true and consistent, here even naïve, exhibits to us openly the inner significance of the act of generation. Our own consciousness, the intensity of the impulse, teaches us that in this act the most decided *assertion of the will to live* expresses itself, pure and without further addition (any denial of other individuals); and now, as the consequence of this act, a new life appears in time and the causal series, *i.e.*, in Nature; the begotten appears before the begetter, different as regards the phenomenon, but in himself, *i.e.*, according to the Idea, identical with him. Therefore it is this act through which every species of living creature binds itself to a whole and is perpetuated. Generation is, with reference to the begetter, only the expression, the symptom, of his decided assertion of the will to live: with reference to the begotten, it is not the cause of the will which appears in him, for the will in itself knows neither cause nor effect, but, like all causes, it is merely the occasional cause of the phenomenal appearance of this will at this time in this place. As thing-in-itself, the will of the begetter and that of the begotten are not different, for only the phenomenon, not the thing-in-itself, is subordinate to the *principium individuationis*. With that assertion beyond our own body and extending to the production of a new body, suffering and death, as belonging to the phenomenon of life, have also been asserted anew, and the possibility of salvation, introduced by the completest capability of knowledge, has for this time been shown to be fruitless. Here lies the profound reason of the shame connected with the process of generation. This view is mythically expressed in the dogma of Christian theology that we are all partakers in Adam's first transgression (which is clearly just the satisfaction of sexual passion), and through it are guilty of suffering and death. In this theology goes beyond the consideration of things according to the principle of sufficient reason, and recognizes the Idea of man, the unity of which is re-established out of its dispersion into unnumerable individuals through the bond of generation which holds them all together. Accordingly it regards every individual as on one side identical with Adam, the representative to the assertion of life, and, so far, as subject to sin (original sin), suffering and death; on the other side, the knowledge of the Idea of man enables it to regard every individual as identical with the saviour, the representative of the denial of the will to live, and, so far as a partaker of his sacrifice of himself, saved through his merits, and delivered from the bands of sin and death, *i.e.*, the world (Rom. v. 12-21).

The sexual impulse also proves itself the decided and strongest assertion of life by the fact that to man in a state of Nature, as to the brutes, it is the final end, the highest goal of life. Self-maintenance is his first effort, and as soon as he has made provision for that, he only strives after the propagation of the species: as a merely natural being he can attempt no more. Nature also, the inner being of which is the will to live itself, impels with all her power both man and the brute towards propagation. Then it has attained its end with the individual, and is quite indifferent to its death, for, as the will to live, it cares only for the preservation of the species, the individual is nothing to it. The genital organs are, far more than any other external member of the body, subject merely to the will, and not at all to knowledge. Indeed, the will shows itself here almost as independent of knowledge, as in those parts which, acting merely in consequence of stimuli, are subservient to vegetative life and reproduction, in which the will works blindly as in unconscious Nature. For generation is only reproduction passing over to a new individual, as it were reproduction at the second power, as death is only excretion at the second power. According to all this, the genitals are properly the *focus* of will, and consequently the opposite pole of the brain, the representative of knowledge, *i.e.*, the other side of the world, the world as idea. The former are the life-sustaining principle ensuring endless life to time. In this respect they were worshiped by the Greeks in the *phallus*, and by the Hindus in the *lingam*, which are thus the symbol of the assertion of the will. Knowledge, on the other hand, affords the possibility of the suppression of willing, of salvation through freedom, of conquest and annihilation of the world.

❖

We have called time and space the *principium individuationis,* because only through them and in them is multiplicity of the homogeneous possible. They are the essential forms of natural knowledge, *i.e.,* knowledge springing from the will. Therefore the will everywhere manifests itself in the multiplicity of individuals. But this multiplicity does not concern the will as thing-in-itself, but only its phenomena. The will itself is present, whole and undivided, in every one of these, and beholds around it the innumerably repeated image of its own nature; but this nature itself, the actually real, it finds directly only in its inner self. Therefore everyone desires everything for himself, desires to possess, or at least to control, everything, and whatever opposes it, it would like to destroy. To this is added, in the case of such beings as have knowledge, that the individual is the supporter of the knowing subject, and the knowing subject is the supporter of the world, *i.e.*, that the whole of Nature outside of knowing subject, and thus also all other individuals, exist only in its idea; it is only conscious of them as its idea, thus merely indirectly as something which is dependent on its own nature and existence; for with its consciousness the world necessarily disappears for it, *i.e.*, its being and non-being become synonymous and indistinguishable. Every knowing individual is thus in truth, and finds itself as the whole will to live, or the inner being of the world itself, and also as the complemental condition of the world as idea, consequently as a microcosm which is of equal value with the macrocosm. Nature itself, which is everywhere and always truthful, gives him this knowledge, originally and independently of all reflection, with simple and direct certainty. Now from these two necessary properties we have given the fact may be explained that every individual, though vanishing altogether and diminished to nothing in the boundless world, yet makes itself the centre of the world, has regard for its own existence and well-being before everything else; indeed, from the natural standpoint, is ready to sacrifice everything else for this—is ready to annihilate the world in order to maintain its own self, this drop in the ocean, a little longer. This disposition is *egoism*, which is essential to everything in Nature. Yet it is just through egoism that the inner conflict of the will with itself attains to such a terrible revelation; for this egoism has its continuance and being in that opposition of the microcosm and macrocosm, or in the fact that the objectification of will has the *principium individuationis* for its form, through which the will manifests itself in the same way in innumerable individuals, and indeed entire and completely in both aspects (will and idea) in each. Thus, while each individual is given to itself directly as the whole will and the whole subject of ideas, other individuals are only given it as ideas. Therefore its own being, and the maintenance of it, is of more importance to it than that of all others together. Everyone looks upon his own death as upon the end of the world, while he accepts the death of his acquaintances as a matter of comparative indifference, if he is not in some way affected by it. In the consciousness that has reached the highest grade, that of man, egoism, as well as knowledge, pain and pleasure, must have reached its highest grade also, and the conflict of individuals which is conditioned by it must appear in its most terrible form. And indeed we see this everywhere before our eyes, in small things as in great.

Now we see its terrible side in the lives of great tyrants and miscreants, and in world-desolating wars; now its absurd side, in which it is the theme of comedy, and very specially appears as self-conceit and vanity. Rochefoucault understood this better than anyone else, and presented it in the abstract. We see it both in the history of the world and in our own experience. But it appears most distinctly of all when any mob of men is set free from all law and order; then there shows itself at once in the distinctest form the *bellum omnium contra omnes*, which Hobbes has so admirably described in the first chapter of *De Cive*. We see not only how everyone tries to seize from the other what he wants himself, but how often one will destroy the whole happiness or life of another for the sake of an insignificant addition to his own happiness. This is the highest expression of egoism, the manifestations of which in this regard are only surpassed by those of actual wickedness, which seeks, quite disinterestedly, the hurt and suffering of others, without any advantage to itself.

But the one end of the *law* is *deterrence* from the infringement of the rights of others. For, in order that everyone may be protected from suffering wrong, men have combined to form a state, have renounced the doing of wrong, and assumed the task of maintaining the state. Thus the law and the fulfilment of it, the punishment, are essentially directed to the *future*, not to the *past*. This distinguishes *punishment* from *revenge;* for the motives which instigate the latter are solely concerned with what has happened, and thus with the past as such. All requital of wrong by the infliction of pain, without any aim of the future, is revenge, and can have no other end than consolation for the suffering one has borne by the sight of the suffering one has inflicted upon another. This is wickedness and cruelty, and cannot be morally justified. Wrong which someone has inflicted upon me by no means entitles me to inflict wrong upon him. Nay, this would rather be the most presumptuous arrogance; and therefore the Bible says, "Vengeance is mine; I will repay, saith the Lord." But man has the right to care for the safety of society.

The world, in all the multiplicity of its parts and forms, is the manifestation, the objectivity, of the one will to live. Existence itself, and the kind of existence, both as a collective whole and in every part, proceeds from the will alone. The will is free, the will is almighty. The will appears in everything, just as it determines itself in itself and outside time. The world is only the mirror of this willing; and all finitude, all suffering, all miseries, which it contains, belong to the expression of that which the will wills, are as they are because the will so wills. Accordingly with perfect right every being supports existence in general, and also the existence of its species and its peculiar individuality, entirely as it is and in circumstances as they are, in a world such as it is, swayed by chance and error, transient, ephemeral, and constantly suffering; and in all that it experiences, or indeed can experience, it always gets its due. For the will belongs to it; and as the will is, so is the world. Only this world itself can bear the responsibility of its own existence and nature—no other; for by what means could another have assumed it? Do we desire to know what men, morally considered, are worth as a whole and in general, we have only to consider their fate as a whole and in general. This is want, wretchedness, affliction, misery, and death. Eternal justice reigns; if they were not, as a whole, worthless, their fate, as a whole, would not be so sad. In this sense we may say, the world itself is the judgment of the world. If we could lay all the misery of the world in one scale of the balance, and all the guilt of the world in the other, the needle would certainly point to the centre.

Certainly, however, the world does not exhibit itself to the knowledge of the individual as such, developed for the service of the will, as it finally reveals itself to the inquirer as the objectivity of the one and only will to live, which he himself is. But the sight of the uncultured individual is clouded, as the Hindus say, by the veil of Maya. He sees not the thing-in-itself but the phenomenon in time and space, the *principium individuationis*, and in the other forms of the principle of sufficient reason. And in this form of his limited knowledge he sees not the inner nature of things, which is one, but its phenomena as separated, disunited, innumerable, very different, and indeed opposed. For to him, pleasure appears as one thing and pain as quite another thing: one man as a tormentor and a murderer, another as a martyr and a victim; wickedness as one thing and evil as another. He sees one man live in joy, abundance and pleasure, and even at his door another die miserably of want and cold. Then he asks, where is the retribution? And he himself in the vehement pressure of will which is his origin and his nature, seizes upon the pleasures and enjoyments of life, firmly embraces them, and knows not that by this very act of his will he seizes and hugs all those pains and sorrows at the sight of which he shudders. He sees the ills and he sees the wickedness in the world, but far from knowing that both of these are but different sides of the manifestation of the one will to live, he regards them as very different, and indeed quite opposed, and often seeks to escape by wickedness, *i.e.*, by causing the suffering of another, from ills, from the suffering of his own individuality, for he is involved in the *principium individuationis*, deluded by the veil of Maya. Just as a sailor sits in a boat trusting to his frail barque in a stormy sea, unbounded in every direction, rising and falling with the howling mountainous waves; so in the midst of a world of sorrows the individual man sits quietly, supported by and trusting to the *principium individuationis*, or the way in which the individual knows things as phenomena. The boundless world, everywhere full of suffering in the infinite past, in the infinite future, is strange to him, indeed is to him but a fable; his ephemeral person, his extensionless present, his momentary satisfaction, this alone has reality for him; and he does all to maintain this, so long as his eyes are not opened by a better knowledge. Till then, there lives only in the inmost depths of his consciousness a very obscure presentiment that all that is after all not really so strange to him, but has a connection with him, from which the *principium individuationis* cannot protect him. From this presentiment arises that ineradicable *awe* common to all men (and indeed perhaps even to the most sensible of the brutes) which suddenly seizes them if by any chance they become puzzled about the *principium individuationis*, because the principle of sufficient reason in some one of its forms seems to admit of an exception. For example, if it seems as if some change took place without a cause, or someone who is dead appears again, or if in any other way the past or the future becomes present or the distant becomes near. The fearful terror at anything of the kind is founded on the fact that they suddenly become puzzled about the forms of knowledge of the phenomenon, which alone separate their own individuality from the rest of the world. But even this separation lies only in the phenomenon, and not in the thing-in-itself; and on this rests eternal justice. According to the true nature of things, everyone has all the suffering of the world as his own, and indeed has to regard all merely possible suffering as for him actual, so long as he has the fixed will to live, *i.e.,* asserts life with all his power. For the knowledge that sees through the *principium individuationis*, a happy life in time, the gift of chance or won by prudence, amid the sorrows of innumerable others, is only the dream of a beggar in which he is a king, but from which he must awake and learn from experience that only a fleeting illusion had separated him from the suffering of his life.

The living knowledge of eternal justice, of the balance that inseparably binds together the *malum culpæ* with the *malum pænæ*, demands the complete transcending of individuality and the principle of its possibility. Therefore it will always remain unattainable to the majority of men, as will also be the case with the pure and distinct knowledge of the nature of all virtue, which is akin to it, and which we are about to explain. Accordingly the wise ancestors of the Hindu people have directly expressed it in the Vedas, which are only allowed to the three regenerate castes, or in their esoteric teaching, so far at any rate as conception and language comprehend it, and their method of exposition, which always remains pictorial and even rhapsodical, admits; but in the religion of the people, or exoteric teaching, they only communicate it by means of myths. The direct exposition we find in the Vedas, the fruit of the highest human knowledge and wisdom, the kernel of which has at last reached us in the Upanishads as the greatest gift of this century. It is expressed in various ways, but especially by making all the beings in the world, living and lifeless, pass successively before the view of the student, and pronouncing over every one of them that word which has become a formula, and as such has been called the Mahavakya: Tatoumes—more correctly, Tat twam asi—which means, "This thou art."

A theory of morals without proof, that is, mere moralizing, can effect nothing, because it does not act as a motive. A theory of morals which does act as a motive can do so only by working on self-love. But what springs from this source has no moral worth. It follows from this that no genuine virtue can be produced through moral theory or abstract knowledge in general, but that such virtue must spring from that intuitive knowledge which recognizes in the individuality of others the same nature as in our own. Thus genuine goodness of disposition, disinterested virtue, and pure nobility do not proceed from abstract knowledge. Yet they do proceed from knowledge; but it is a direct intuitive knowledge, which can neither be reasoned away, nor arrived at by reasoning, a knowledge which, just because it is not abstract, cannot be communicated, but must arise in each for himself, which therefore finds its real and adequate expression not in words, but only in deeds, in conduct, in the course of the life of man.

However closely the veil of Maya may envelop the mind of the bad man, *i.e.*, however firmly he may be involved in the *principium individuationis*, according to which he regards his person as absolutely different and separated by a wide gulf from all others, a knowledge to which he clings with all his might, as it alone suits and supports his egoism, so that knowledge is almost always corrupted by will, yet there arises in the inmost depths of his consciousness the secret presentiment that such an order of things is only phenomenal, and that their real constitution is quite different. He has a dim foreboding that, however much time and space may separate him from other individuals and the innumerable miseries which they suffer, and even suffer through him, and may represent them as quite foreign to him, yet in themselves, and apart from the idea and its forms, it is the one will to live appearing in them all, which here failing to recognize itself, turns its weapons against itself, and, by seeking increased happiness in one of its phenomena, imposes the greatest suffering upon another. He dimly sees that he, the bad man, is himself this whole will; that consequently he is not only the inflicter of pain but also the endurer of it, from whose suffering he in only separated and exempted by an illusive dream, the form of which is space and time, which, however, vanishes away; that he must in reality pay for the pleasure with the pain, and that all suffering which he only knows as possible really concerns him as the will to live, inasmuch as the possible and actual, the near and the distant in time and space, are only different for the knowledge of the individual, only by means of the *principium individuationis,* not in themselves. This is the truth which mythically, *i.e.,* adapted to the principle of sufficient reason, and so translated into the form of the phenomenal, is expressed in the transmigration of souls. Yet it has its purest expression, free from all foreign admixture, in that obscurely felt yet inconsolable misery called remorse.

If, however, as a rare exception, we meet a man who possesses a considerable income, but uses very little of it for himself and gives all the rest to the poor, while he denies himself many pleasures and comforts, and we seek to explain the action of this man, we shall find, apart altogether from the dogmas through which he tries to make his action intelligible to his reason, that the simplest general expression and the essential character of his conduct is that *he makes less distinction than is usually made between himself and others.* This distinction is so great in the eyes of many that the suffering of others is a direct pleasure to the wicked and a welcome means of happiness to the unjust. The merely just man is content not to cause it; and, in general, most men know and are acquainted with innumerable sufferings of others in their vicinity, but do not determine to mitigate them, because to do so would involve some self-denial on their part. Thus, in each of all these a strong distinction seems to prevail between his own ego and that of others; on the other hand, to the noble man we have imagined, this distinction is not so significant. The *principium individuationis*, the form of the phenomenon, no longer holds him so tightly in its grasp, but the suffering which he sees in others touches him almost as closely as his own. He therefore tries to strike a balance between them, denies himself pleasures, practises renunciation, in order to mitigate the sufferings of others. He sees that the distinction between himself and others, which to the bad man is so great a gulf, only belongs to a fleeting and illusive phenomenon. He recognizes directly and without reasoning that the in-itself of his own manifestation is also that of others, the will to live, which constitutes the inner nature of everything and lives in all; indeed, that this applies also to the brutes and the whole of Nature, and therefore he will not cause suffering even to a brute.

But before I go further, and, as the conclusion of my exposition, show how love, the origin and nature of which we recognized as the penetration of the *principium individuationis*, leads to salvation, to the entire surrender of the will to live, *i.e.*, of all volition, and also how another path, less soft but more frequented, leads men to the same goal, a paradoxical proposition must first be stated and explained; not because it is paradoxical, but because it is true, and is necessary to the completeness of the thought I have present. It is this: "All love (ἀγάπη, *caritas*) is sympathy." The mere concept is for genuine virtue just as unfruitful as it is for genuine art: all true and pure love is sympathy, and all love which is not sympathy is selfishness. "Ερως is selfishness, ἀγάπη is sympathy. Combinations of the two frequently occur. Indeed genuine friendship is always a mixture of selfishness and sympathy; the former lies in the pleasure experienced in the presence of the friend, whose individuality corresponds to our own, and this almost always constitutes the greatest part; sympathy shows itself in the sincere participation in his joy and grief, and the disinterested sacrifices made in respect of the latter. Thus Spinoza says: *Benevolentia nihil aliud est, quam cupiditas ex commiseratione orta* (Eth. Iii. pr. 27, cor. 3, schol.). As a confirmation of our paradoxical proposition it may be observed that the tone and words of the language and caresses of pure love, entirely coincide with the tones of sympathy; and we may also remark in passing that in Italian, sympathy and true love are denoted by the same word *pietà*.

We saw before that hatred and wickedness are conditioned by egoism, and egoism rests on the entanglement of knowledge in the *principium individuationis*. Thus we found that the penetration of that *principium individuationis* is the source and the nature of justice, and when it is carried further, even to its fullest extent, it is the source and nature of love and nobility of character. For this penetration alone, by abolishing the distinction between our own individuality and that of others, renders possible and explains perfect goodness of disposition, extending to disinterested love and the most generous self-sacrifice for others.

If, however, this penetration of the *principium individuationis*, this direct knowledge of the identity of will in all its manifestations, is present in a high degree of distinctness, it will at once show an influence upon the will which extends still further. If that veil of Maya, the *principium individuationis*, is lifted from the eyes of a man to such an extent that he no longer makes the egotistical distinction between his person and that of others, but takes as much interest in the sufferings of other individuals as in his own, and therefore is not only benevolent in the highest degree, but even ready to sacrifice his own individuality whenever such a sacrifice will save a number of other persons, then it clearly follows that such a man, who recognizes in all beings his own inmost and true self, must also regard the infinite suffering of all suffering beings as his own, and take on himself the pain of the whole world. No suffering is any longer strange to him. All the miseries of others which he sees and is so seldom able to alleviate, all the miseries he knows directly, and even those which he only knows as possible, work upon his mind like his own. It is no longer the changing joy and sorrow of his own person that he has in view, as is the case with him who is still involved in egoism; but, since he sees through the *principium individuationis*, all lies equally near him. He knows the whole, comprehends its nature, and finds that it consists in a constant passing away, vain striving, inward conflict and continual suffering. He sees wherever he looks suffering humanity, the suffering brute creation and a world that passes away. But all this now lies as near him as him own person lies to the egoist. Why should he now, with such knowledge of the world, assert this very life through constant acts of will, and thereby bind himself ever more closely to it, press it ever more firmly to himself? Thus he who is still involved in the *principium individuationis*, in egoism, only knows particular things and their relation to his own person, and these constantly become new *motives* of his volition. But, on the other hand, that knowledge of the whole, of the nature of the thing-in-itself which has been described, becomes a *quieter* of all and every volition. The *will* now turns away from life; it now shudders at the pleasures in which it recognizes the assertion of life. Man now attains to the state of voluntary renunciation, resignation, true indifference and perfect will-lessness.

If we compare life to a course or path through which we must unceasingly run—a path of red-hot coals, with a few cool places here and there; then he who is entangled in delusion is consoled by the cool places, on which he now stands, or which he sees near him, and sets out to run through the course. But he who sees through the *principium individuationis*, and recognizes the real nature of the thing-in-itself, and thus the whole, is no longer susceptible of such consolation; he sees himself in all places at once, and withdraws. His will turns round, no longer asserts its own nature, which is reflected in the phenomenon, but denies it. The phenomenon by which this change is marked, is the transition from virtue to asceticism. That is to say, it no longer suffices for such a man to love others as himself, and to do as much for them as for himself; but there arises within him a horror of the nature of which his own phenomenal existence is an expression, the will to live, the kernel and inner nature of that world which is recognized as full of misery. He therefore disowns this nature which appears in him, and is already expressed through his body, and his action gives the lie to his phenomenal existence, and appears in open contradiction to it. Essentially nothing else but a manifestation of will, he ceases to will anything, guards against attaching his will to anything, and seeks to confirm in himself the greatest indifference to everything. His body, healthy and strong, expresses through the genitals, the sexual impulse; but he denies the will and gives the lie to the body; he desires no sensual gratification under any condition. Voluntary and complete chastity is the first step in asceticism or the denial of the will to live. It thereby denies the assertion of the will which extends beyond the individual life, and gives the assurance that with the life of this body, the will, whose manifestation it is, ceases. Nature, always true and naïve, declares that if this maxim became universal, the human race would die out; and I think I may assume, in accordance with what was said in the Second Book about the connection of all manifestations of will, that with its highest manifestation, the weaker reflection of it would also pass away, as the twilight vanishes along with the full light. With the entire abolition of knowledge, the rest of the world would of itself vanish into nothing; for without a subject there is no object. I should like here to refer to a passage in the Vedas, where it is said: "As in this world hungry infants press round their mother; so do all beings await the holy oblation." (*Asiatic Researches*, vol. viii.; Colebrooke, *On the Vedas, Abstract of the Sama-Veda*; also in Colebrooke's *Miscellaneous Essays*, vol. i. p. 79.) Sacrifice means resignation generally, and the rest of Nature must look for its salvation to man who is at once the priest and the sacrifice. Indeed it deserves to be noticed as very remarkable, that this thought has also been expressed by the admirable and unfathomably profound Angelus Silesius, in the little poem entitled, "Man brings all to God"; it runs:

"Man! all loves thee; around thee; around thee great is the throng. All things flee to thee that they may attain to God."

The history of the world will, and indeed must, keep silence about the men whose conduct is the best and only adequate illustration of this important point of our investigation, for the material of the history of the world is quite different, and indeed opposed to this. It is not the denial of the will to live, but its assertion and its manifestation in innumerable individuals in which its conflict with itself at the highest grade of its objectification appears with perfect distinctness, and brings before our eyes, now the ascendancy of the individual through prudence, now the might of the many through their mass, now the might of chance personified as fate, always the vanity and emptiness of the whole effort. We, however, do not follow here the course of phenomena in time, but, as philosophers, we seek to investigate the ethical significance of action, and take this as the only criterion of what for us is significant and important. Thus we will not be withheld by any fear of the constant numerical superiority of vulgarity and dullness from acknowledging that the greatest, most important, and most significant phenomenon that the world can show is not the conqueror of the world, but the subduer of it; is nothing but the quiet, unobserved life of a man who has attained to the knowledge in consequence of which he surrenders and denies that will to live which fills everything and strives and strains in all, and which first gains freedom here in him alone, so that his conduct becomes the exact opposite of that of other men. In this respect, therefore, for the philosopher, these accounts of the lives of holy, self-denying men, badly as they are generally written, and mixed as they are with superstitition and nonsense, are, because of the significance of the material, immeasurably more instructive and important than even Plutarch and Livy.

We saw above that the wicked man, by the vehemence of his volition, suffers constant, consuming, inward pain, and finally, if all objects of volition are exhausted, quenches the fiery thirst of his self-will by the sight of the suffering of others. He, on the contrary, who has attained to the denial of the will to live, however poor, joyless, and full of privation his condition may appear when looked at externally, is yet filled with inward joy and the true peace of heaven. It is not the restless strain of life, the jubilant delight which has keen suffering as its preceding or succeeding condition, in the experience of the man who loves life; but it is a peace that cannot be shaken, a deep rest and inward serenity, a state which we cannot behold without the greatest longing when it is brought before our eyes or our imagination, because we at once recognize it as that which alone is right, infinitely surpassing everything else, upon which our better self cries within us the great *sapere aude*. Then we feel that every gratification of our wishes won from the world is merely like the alms which the beggar receives from life today that he may hunger again on the morrow; resignation, on the contrary, is like an inherited estate, it frees the owner for ever from all care.

It will be remembered from the Third Book that the æsthetic pleasure in the beautiful consists in great measure the fact that in entering the state of pure contemplation we are lifted for the moment above all willing, *i.e.*, all wishes and cares; we become, as it were, freed from ourselves. We are no longer the individual whose knowledge is subordinated to the service of its constant willing, the correlative of the particular thing to which objects are motives, but the eternal subject of knowing purified from will, the correlative of the Platonic Idea. And we know that these moments in which, delivered from the ardent strain of will, we seem to rise out of the heavy atmosphere of earth, are the happiest which we experience. From this we can understand how blessed the life of a man must be whose will is silenced, not merely for a moment, as in the enjoyment of the beautiful, but for ever, indeed altogether extinguished, except as regards the last glimmering spark that retains the body in life, and will be extinguished with its death. Such a man, who, after many bitter struggles with his own nature, has finally conquered entirely, continues to exist only as a pure, knowing being, the undimmed mirror of the world. Nothing can trouble him more, nothing can move him, for he has cut all the thousand cords of will which hold us bound to the world, and, as desire, fear, envy, anger, drag us hither and thither in constant pain. He now looks back smiling and at rest on the delusions of this world, which once were able to move and agonize his spirit also, but which now stand before him as utterly indifferent to him, as the chess-men when the game is ended, or as, in the morning, the cast-off masquerading dress which worried and disquieted us in a night in Carnival. Life and its forms now pass before him as a fleeting illusion, as a light morning dream before half-waking eyes, the real world already shining through it so that it can no longer deceive; and like this morning dream, they finally vanish altogether without any violent transition.

In this sense, then, the old philosophical doctrine of the freedom of the will, which has constantly been contested and constantly maintained, is not without ground, and the dogma of the Church of the work of grace and the new birth is not without meaning and significance. But we now unexpectedly see both united in one, and we can also now understand in what sense the excellent Malebranche could say, *"La liberté est un mystère,"* and was right. For precisely what the Christian mystics call *the work of grace* and *the new birth*, is for us the single direct expression of *the freedom of the will*. It only appears if the will, having attained to a knowledge of its own real nature, receives from this a *quieter,* by means of which the motives are deprived of their effect, which belongs to the province of another kind of knowledge, the objects of which are merely phenomena. The possibility of the freedom which thus expresses itself is the greatest prerogative of man, which is for ever wanting to the brute, because the condition of it is the deliberation of reason, which enables him to survey the whole of life independent of the impression of the present. The brute is entirely without the possibility of freedom, as, indeed, it is without the possibility of a proper or deliberate choice following upon a completed conflict of motives, which for this purpose would have to be abstract ideas. Therefore with the same necessity with which the stone falls to the earth, the hungry wolf buries its fangs in the flesh of its prey, without the possibility of the knowledge that it is itself the destroyed as well as the destroyer. *Necessity is the kingdom of nature; freedom is the kingdom of grace.*

If, however, it should be absolutely insisted upon that in some way or other a positive knowledge should be attained of that which philosophy can only express negatively as the denial of the will, there would be nothing for it but to refer to that state which all those who have attained to complete denial of the will have experienced, and which has been variously denoted by the names ecstasy, rapture, illumination union with God and so forth; a state, however, which cannot properly be called knowledge, because it has not the form of subject and object, and is, moreover, only attainable in one's own experience and cannot be further communicated.

We, however, who consistently occupy the standpoint of philosophy, must be satisfied here with negative knowledge, content to have reached the utmost limit of the positive. We have recognized the inmost nature of the world as will, and all its phenomena as only the objectivity of will; and we have followed this objectivity from the unconscious working of obscure forces of Nature up to the completely conscious action of man. Therefore we shall by no means evade the consequence, that with the free denial, the surrender of the will, all those phenomena are also abolished; that constant strain and effort without end and without rest at all the grades of objectivity, in which and through which the world consists; the multifarious forms succeeding each other in gradation; the whole manifestation of the will; and, finally, also the universal forms of this manifestation, time and space, and also its last fundamental form, subject and object; all are abolished. No will: no idea, no world.

Before us there is certainly only nothingness. But that which resists this passing into nothing, our nature, is indeed just the will to live, which we ourselves are as it is our world. That we abhor annihilation so greatly, is simply another expression of the fact that we so strenuously will life, and are nothing but this will, and know nothing besides it. But if we turn our glance from our own needy and embarrassed condition to those who have overcome the world, in whom the will, having attained to perfect self-knowledge, found itself again in all, and then freely denied itself, and who then merely wait to see the last trace of it vanish with the body which it animates; then, instead of the restless striving and effort, instead of the constant transition from wish to fruition, and from joy to sorrow, instead of the never-satisfied and never-dying hope which constitutes the life of the man who wills, we shall see that peace which is above all reason, that perfect calm of the spirit, that deep rest, that inviolable confidence and serenity, the mere reflection of which in the countenance, as Raphael and Correggio have represented it, is an entire and certain gospel; only knowledge remains, the will has vanished. We look with deep and painful longing upon this state, beside which the misery and wretchedness of our own is brought out clearly by the contrast. Yet this is the only consideration which can afford us lasting consolation, when, on the one hand, we have recognized incurable suffering and endless misery as essential to the manifestation of will, the world; and, on the other hand, see the world pass away with the abolition of will, and retain before us only empty nothingness. Thus, in this way, by contemplation of the life and conduct of saints, whom it is certainly rarely granted us to meet with in our own experience, but who are brought before our eyes by their written history, and, with the stamp of inner truth, by art, we must banish the dark impression of that nothingness which we discern behind all virtue and holiness as their final goal, and which we fear as children fear the dark; we must not even evade it like the Indians, through myths and meaningless words, such as reabsorption in Brahma or the Nirvana of the Buddhists. Rather do we freely acknowledge that what remains after the entire abolition of will is for all those who are still full of will certainly nothing; but, conversely, to those in whom the will has turned and has denied itself, this our world, which is so real, with all its suns and milky-ways—is nothing.

In boundless space countless shining spheres, about each of which, and illuminated by its light, there revolve a dozen or so of smaller ones, hot at the core and covered with a hard, cold crust, upon whose surface there have been generated from a mouldy film beings which live and know—this is what presents itself to us in experience as the truth, the real, the world. Yet for a thinking being it is a precarious position to stand upon one of those numberless spheres moving freely in boundless space without knowing whence or whither, and to be only one of innumerable similar beings who throng and press and toil, ceaselessly and quickly arising and passing away in time, which has no beginning and no end; moreover, nothing permanent but matter alone and the recurrence of the same varied organized forms, by means of certain ways and channels which are there once for all. All that empirical science can teach is only the more exact nature and law of these events. But now at last modern philosophy, especially through Berkeley and Kant, has called to mind that all this is first of all merely a *phenomenon of the brain,* and is affected with such great, so many, and such different *subjective* conditions that its supposed absolute reality vanishes away, and leaves room for an entirely different scheme of the world, which consists of what lies at the foundation of that phenomenon, *i.e.,* what is related to it as the thing in itself is related to its mere manifestation.

"The world is my idea" is, like the axioms of Euclid, a proposition which everyone must recognize as true as soon as he understands it; although it is not a proposition which everyone understands as soon as he hears it. To have brought this proposition to clear consciousness, and in it the problem of the relation of the ideal and the real, *i.e.,* of the world in the head to the world outside the head, together with the problem of moral freedom, is the distinctive feature of modern philosophy. For it was only after men had spent their labour for thousands of years upon a mere philosophy of the object that they discovered that among the many things that make the world so obscure and doubtful the first and chiefest is this, that however immeasurable and massive it may be, its existence yet hangs by a single thread; and this is the actual consciousness in which it exists. This condition, to which the existence of the world is irrevocably subject, marks it, in spite of all *empirical* reality, with the stamp of *ideality,* and therefore of mere *phenomenal appearance.* Thus on one side at least the world must be recognized as akin to dreams, and indeed to be classified along with them. For the same function of the brain which, during sleep, conjures up before us a completely objective, perceptible and even palpable world must have just as large a share in the presentation of the objective world of waking life. Both worlds, although different as regards their matter, are yet clearly moulded in the one form. This form is the intellect, the function of the brain.

Thus true philosophy must always be idealistic; indeed, it must be so in order to be merely honest. For nothing is more certain than that no man ever came out of himself in order to identify himself directly with things which are different from him; but everything of which he has certain, and therefore immediate, knowledge lies within his own consciousness. Beyond this consciousness, therefore, there can be no *immediate* certainty; but the first principles of a science must have such certainty. For the empirical standpoint of the other sciences it is quite right to assume the objective world as something absolutely given; but not so for the standpoint of philosophy, which has to go back to what is first and original. Only consciousness is immediately given; therefore the basis of philosophy is limited to facts of consciousness, *i.e.*, it is essentially *idealistic*.

With the exception of man, no being wonders at its own existence; but it is to them all so much a matter of course that they do not observe it. The wisdom of Nature speaks out of the peaceful glance of the brutes; for in them the will and the intellect are not yet so widely separated that they can be astonished at each other when they meet again. Thus here the whole phenomenon is still firmly attached to the stem of nature from which it has come, and is partaker of the unconscious omniscience of the great mother. Only after the inner being of nature (the will to live in its objectification) has ascended, vigorous and cheerful, through the two series of unconscious existences, and then through the long and broad series of animals, does it attain at last to reflection for the first time on the entrance of reason, thus in man. Then it marvels at its own works, and asks itself what it itself is. Its wonder, however, is the more serious, as it here stands for the first time consciously in the presence of *death*, and besides the finiteness of all existence, the vanity of all effort forces itself more or less upon it. With this reflection and this wonder there arises, therefore, for man alone the *need for a metaphysic;* he is accordingly an *animal metaphysicum.* At the beginning of his consciousness certainly he also accepts himself as a matter of course. This does not last long, however, but very early, with the first dawn of reflection, that wonder already appears, which is some day to become the mother of metaphysics. In agreement with this Aristotle also says at the beginning of his metaphysics: "Διὰ γὰρ τὸ θανμάζειν οἱ ἄνθρωποι καὶ τὸ πρῶτον ἤρξαντο φιλοσοφεῖν." (*Propter admirationem enim et nunc et primo inceperunt homines philosophari.*) Moreover, the special philosophical disposition consists primarily in this, that a man is capable of wonder beyond the ordinary and everyday degree, and is thus induced to make the *universal* of the phenomenon his problem, while the investigators in the natural sciences wonder only at exquisite or rare phenomena, and their problem is merely to refer these to phenomena which are better known. The lower a man stands in an intellectual regard the less of a problem is existence itself for him; everything, how it is and that it is, appears to him rather a matter of course. This rests upon the fact that his intellect still remains perfectly true to its original destiny of being serviceable to the will as the medium of motives, and therefore is closely bound up with the world and nature, as an integral part of them. Consequently it is very far from comprehending the world in a purely objective manner, freeing itself, so to speak, from the whole of things, opposing itself to this whole, and so for a while becoming as if self-existent. On the other hand, the philosophical wonder which springs from this is conditioned in the individual by higher development of the intellect, yet in general not by this alone; but without doubt it is the knowledge of death, and along with this the consideration of the suffering and misery of life, which gives the strongest impulse to philosophical reflection and metaphysical explanation of the world. If our life were endless and painless, it would perhaps occur to no one to ask why the world exists, and is just the kind of world it is; but everything would just be taken as a matter of course. In accordance with this we find that the interest which philosophical and also religious systems inspire has always its strongest hold in the dogma of some kind of existence after death; and although the most recent systems seem to make the existence of their gods the main point, and to defend this most zealously, yet in reality this is only because they have connected their special dogma of immortality with this, and regard the one as inseparable from the other: only on this account is it of importance to them.

Temples and churches, pagodas and mosques, in all lands and in all ages, in splendour and vastness, testify to the metaphysical need of man, which, strong and ineradicable, follows close upon his physical need. Certainly whoever is satirically inclined might add that this metaphysical need is a modest fellow who is content with poor fare. It sometimes allows itself to be satisfied with clumsy fables and insipid tales. If only imprinted early enough, they are for a man adequate explanations of his existence and supports of his morality. Consider, for example, the Koran. This wretched book was sufficient to found a religion of the world, to satisfy the metaphysical need of innumerable millions of men for twelve hundred years, to become the foundation of their morality, and of no small contempt for death, and also to inspire them to bloody wars and most extended conquests. We find in it the saddest and the poorest form of Theism. Much may be lost through the translations; but I have not been able to discover one single valuable thought in it. Such things show that metaphysical capacity does not go hand in hand with the metaphysical need. Yet it will appear that in the early ages of the present surface of the earth this was not the case, and that those who stood considerably nearer than we do to the beginning of the human race and the source of organic nature, had also both greater energy of the intuitive faculty of knowledge, and a truer disposition of mind, so that they were capable of a purer, more direct comprehension of the inner being of nature, and were thus in a position to satisfy the metaphysical need in a more worthy manner. Thus originated in the primitive ancestors of the Brahmans, the Rishis, the almost superhuman conceptions which were afterwards set down in the Upanishads of the Vedas.

By *metaphysics* I understand all knowledge that pretends to transcend the possibility of experience, thus to transcend Nature or the given phenomenal appearance of things, in order to give an explanation of that by which, in some sense or other, this experience or nature is conditioned; or, to speak in popular language, of that which is behind Nature, and makes it possible. But the great original diversity in the power of understanding, besides the cultivation of it, which demands much leisure, makes so great a difference between men, that as soon as a people has emerged from the state of savages, no *one* metaphysic can serve for them all. Therefore among civilized nations we find throughout two different kinds of metaphysics, which are distinguished by the fact that the one has its evidence *in itself,* the other *outside itself.* Since the metaphysical systems of the first kind require reflection, culture and leisure for the recognition of their evidence, they can be accessible only to a very small number of men; and, moreover, they can only arise and maintain their existence in the case of advanced civilization. On the other hand, the systems of the second kind exclusively are for the great majority of men who are not capable of thinking, but only of believing, and who are not accessible to reason, but only to authority. These systems may therefore be called metaphysics of the people, after the analogy of poetry of the people, and also wisdom of the people, by which is understood proverbs. These systems, however, are known under the name of religions, and are found among all nations, not excepting even the most savage. Their evidence is, as has been said, external, and as such is called revelation, which is authenticated by signs and miracles. Their arguments are principally threats of eternal, and indeed also temporal evils, directed against unbelievers, and even against mere doubters. As *ultima ratio theologorum*, we find among many nations the stake or things similar to it. If they seek a different authentication, or if they make use of other arguments, they already make the transition into the systems of the first kind, and may degenerate into a mixture of the two, which brings more danger than advantage.

To the distinction established above between metaphysics of the first and of the second kind, we have yet to add the following: A system of the first kind, thus a philosophy, makes the claim, and has therefore the obligation, in everything that it says, *sensu stricto et proprio*, to be true, for it appeals to thought and conviction. A religion, on the other hand, being intended for the innumerable multitude who, since they are incapable of examination and thought, would never comprehend the profoundest and most difficult thruths *sensu proprio,* has only the obligation to be true *sensu allegorico*. Truth cannot appear naked before the people. A symptom of this *allegorical* nature of religions is the *mysteries* which are to be found perhaps in all of them, certain dogmas which cannot even be distinctly thought, not to speak of being literally true. Indeed, perhaps it might be asserted that some absolute contradictions, some actual absurdities, are an essential ingredient in a complete religion, for these are just the stamp of its allegorical nature, and the only adequate means of making the ordinary mind and the uncultured understanding *feel* what would be incomprehensible to it, that religion has ultimately to do with quite a different order of things, with an order of *things in themselves,* in the presence of which the laws of this phenomenal world, in conformity with which it must speak, vanish; and that therefore not only the contradictory but also the comprehensible dogmas are really only allegories and accommodations to the human power of comprehension. It seems to me that it was in this spirit that Augustine and even Luther adhered to the mysteries of Christianity in opposition to Pelagianism, which sought to reduce everything to the dull level of comprehensibility. From this point of view it is also conceivable how Tertullian could say in all seriousness: *"Prorsus credibile est, quia ineptum est: ... certum est, quia impossibile"* (*De Carne Christi,* c. 5).

Religions are necessary for the people, and an inestimable benefit to them. But if they oppose themselves to the progress of mankind in the knowledge of the truth, they must with the utmost possible forbearance be set aside. And to require that a great mind—a Shakespeare; a Goethe—should make the dogmas of any religion implicitly, *bona fide et sensu proprio,* his conviction is to require that a giant should put on the shoe of a dwarf.

I cannot place, as is always done, the fundamental difference of all religions in the question whether they are monotheistic, polytheistic, pantheistic or atheistic, but only in the question whether they are optimistic or pessimistic, that is, whether they present the existence of the world as justified by itself, and therefore praise and value it, or regard it as something that can only be conceived as the consequence of our guilt, and therefore properly ought not to be, because they recognize that pain and death cannot lie in the eternal, original and immutable order of things, in that which in every respect ought to be. The power by virtue of which Christianity was able to overcome first Judaism, and then the heathenism of Greece and Rome, lies solely in its pessimism, in the confession that our state is both exceedingly wretched and sinful, while Judaism and heathenism were optimistic. That truth, profoundly and painfully felt by all, penetrated, and bore in its train the need of redemption.

I turn to a general consideration of the other kind of metaphysics, that which has its authentication in itself and is called *philosophy*. I remind the reader of its origin, mentioned above, in a *wonder* concerning the world and our own existence, inasmuch as these press upon the intellect as a riddle, the solution of which therefore occupies mankind without intermission. Here, then, I wish first of all to draw attention to the fact that this could not be the case if, in Spinoza's sense, which in our own day has so often been brought forward again under modern forms and expositions as pantheism, the world were an "*absolute substance*," and therefore an *absolutely necessary existence.* For this means that it exists with so great a necessity that beside it every other necessity comprehensible to our understanding as such must appear as an accident. It would then be something which comprehended in itself not only all actual but also all possible existence, so that, as Spinoza indeed declares, its possibility and its actuality would be absolutely one. Its non-being would therefore be impossibility itself; thus it would be something the non-being or other-being of which must be completely inconceivable, and which could therefore just as little be thought away as, for example, space or time. And since, further, *we ourselves* would be parts, modes, attributes or accidents of such an absolute substance, which would be the only thing that, in any sense, could ever or anywhere exist, our and its existence, together with its properties, would necessarily be very far from presenting itself to us as remarkable, problematical, and indeed as an unfathomable and ever-disquieting riddle, but, on the contrary, would be far more self-evident than that two and two make four. For we would necessarily be incapable of thinking anything else than that the world is, and is, as it is; and therefore we would necessarily be as little conscious of its existence *as such, i.e.,* as a problem for reflection as we are of the incredibly fast motion of our planet.

All this, however, is absolutely not the case. Only to the brutes, who are without thought, does the world and existence appear as a matter of course; to man, on the contrary, it is a problem, of which even the most uneducated and narrow-minded becomes vividly conscious in certain brighter moments, but which enters more distinctly and more permanently into the consciousness of each one of us the clearer and more enlightened that consciousness is, and the more material for thought it has acquired through culture, which all ultimately rises, in minds that are naturally adapted for philosophizing, to Plato's "θαυμάζειν, μάλα φιλοσάφικον πάθος" (*mirari, valde philosophicus affectus*), that is, to that *wonder* which comprehends in its whole magnitude that problem which unceasingly occupies the nobler portion of mankind in every age and in every land, and gives it no rest. In fact, the pendulum which keeps in motion the clock of metaphysics, that never runs down, is the consciousness that the non-existence of this world is just as possible as its existence. Thus, then, the Spinozistic view of it as an absolutely necessary existence, that is, as something that absolutely and in every sense ought to and must be, is a false one. Even simple Theism, since in its cosmological proof it tacitly starts by inferring the previous non-existence of the world from its existence, thereby assumes beforehand that the world is something contingent. Nay, what is more, we very soon apprehend the world as something the non-existence of which is not only conceivable, but indeed preferable to its existence. Therefore our wonder at it easily passes into a brooding over the *fatality* which could yet call forth its existence, and by virtue of which such stupendous power as is demanded for the production and maintenance of such a world could be directed so much against its own interest. The philosophical astonishment is therefore at bottom perplexed and melancholy; philosophy, like the overture to *Don Juan*, commences with a minor chord. It follows from this that it can neither be Spinozism nor optimism. The more special nature, which has just been indicated, of the astonishment which leads us to philosophize clearly springs from the sight of the *suffering and the wickedness* in the world, which, even if they were in the most just proportion to each other, and also were far outweighed by good, are yet something which absolutely and in general ought not to be. But since now nothing can come out of nothing, these also must have their germ in the origin or in the kernel of the world itself. It is hard for us to assume this if we look at the magnitude, the order and completeness, of the physical world, for it seems to us that what had the power to produce such a world must have been able to avoid the suffering and the wickedness. That assumption (the truest expression of which is Ormuzd and Ahrimines), it is easy to conceive, is hardest of all for Theism. Therefore the freedom of the will was primarily invented to account for wickedness. But this is only a concealed way of making something out of nothing, for it assumes an *Operari* that proceeded from no *Esse* (see *Die beiden Grundprobleme der Ethik*, p.58 *et seq.*; second edition, p. 57 *et seq.*). Then it was sought to get rid of evil by attributing it to matter, or to unavoidable necessity, whereby the devil, who is really the right *Expediens ad hoc* was unwillingly set aside. To evil also belongs *death*; but wickedness is only the throwing of the existing evil from oneself on to another. Thus, as was said above, it is wickedness, evil and death that qualify and intensify the philosophical astonishment. Not merely that the world exists, but still more that it is such a wretched world, is the *punctum pruriens* of metaphysics, the problem which awakens in mankind an unrest that cannot be quieted by scepticism nor yet by criticism.

We find *physics* also (in the widest sense of the word) occupied with the explanation of the phenomena in the world. But it lies in the very nature of its explanations themselves that they cannot be sufficient. Physics cannot stand on its own feet, but requires a metaphysic to lean upon, whatever airs it may give itself towards the latter. For it explains the phenomena by something still more unknown than they are themselves; by laws of Nature resting upon forces of Nature, to which the power of life also belongs. With naturalism, then, or the purely physical way of looking at things, we shall never attain our end; it is like a sum that never comes out. Causal series without beginning or end, fundamental forces which are inscrutable, endless space, beginningless time, infinite divisibility of matter, and all this further conditioned by a knowing brain, in which alone it exists just like a dream, and without which it vanishes—constitute the labyrinth in which naturalism leads us ceaselessly round. The height to which in our time the natural sciences have risen in this respect entirely throws into the shade all previous centuries, and is a summit which mankind reaches for the first time. But however great are the advances which *physics* (understood in the wide sense of the ancients) may make, not the smallest step towards *metaphysics* is thereby taken, just as a plane can never obtain cubical content by being indefinitely extended. For all such advances will only perfect our knowledge of the *phenomenon;* while *metaphysics* strives to pass beyond the phenomenal appearance itself, to that which so appears. And if indeed it had the assistance of an entire and complete experience, it would, as regards the main point, be in no way advantaged by it. Nay, even if one wandered through all the planets and fixed stars, one would thereby have made no step in *metaphysics.* It is rather the case that the greatest advances of physics will make the need of metaphysics ever more felt; for it is just the corrected, extended and more thorough knowledge of Nature which, on the one hand, always undermines and ultimately overthrows the metaphysical assumptions which till then have prevailed, but, on the other hand, presents the problem of metaphysics itself more distinctly, more correctly and more fully, and separates it more clearly from all that is merely physical; moreover, the more perfectly and accurately known nature of the particular thing more pressingly demands the explanation of the whole and the general, which, the more correctly, thoroughly and completely it is known empirically, only presents itself as the more mysterious. Certainly the individual, simple investigator of Nature, in a special branch of physics, does not at once become clearly conscious of all this; he rather sleeps contentedly by the side of his chosen maid, in the house of Odysseus, banishing all thoughts of Penelope. Yet, on the other hand, it is to be observed that the most perfect possible knowledge of Nature is the corrected *statement of the problem* of metaphysics. Therefore no one ought to venture upon this without having first acquired a knowledge of all the branches of natural science, which, though general, shall be thorough, clear and connected. For the problem must precede its solution. Then, however, the investigator must turn his glance inward; for the intellectual and ethical phenomena are more important than the physical, in the same proportion as, for example, animal magnetism is a far more important phenomenon than mineral magnetism. The last fundamental secret man carries within himself, and this is accessible to him in the most immediate manner; therefore it is only here that he can hope to find the key to the riddle of the world and gain a clue to the nature of all things. The special province of metaphysics thus certainly lies in what has been called mental philosophy.

The task of metaphysics is certainly not the observation of particular experiences, but yet it is the correct explanation of experience as a whole. Its foundation must therefore, at any rate, be of an empirical nature. Indeed, the *a priori* nature of a part of human knowledge will be apprehended by it as a given *fact*, from which it will infer the subjective origin of the same. Only because the consciousness of its a *priori* nature accompanies it is it called by Kant *transcendental* as distinguished from *transcendent*, which signifies "passing beyond all possibility of experience," and has its opposite in *immanent*, *i.e.*, remaining within the limits of experience. Now, besides this, the source of the knowledge of metaphysics is not *outer* experience alone, but also *inner*. Indeed, what is most peculiar to it, that by which

the decisive step which alone can solve the great question
becomes possible for it, consists, as I have fully and
thoroughly proved in *Ueber den Willen in der Natur,* under
the heading, "Physische Astronomie," in this, that at the
right place it combines outer experience with inner, and
uses the latter as a key to the former. It is neither, according
to the definition of metaphysics which even Kant repeats,
a science of mere conceptions, nor is it a system of
deductions from *a priori* principles, the uselessness of
which for the *end* of metaphysics has been shown by Kant.
But it is rational knowledge, drawn from perception of the
external actual world and the information which the most
intimate fact of self-consciousness affords us concerning
it, deposited in distinct conceptions. It is accordingly the
science of experience; but its subject and its source is not
particular experiences, but the totality of all experience.
I completely accept Kant's doctrine that the world of
experience is merely phenomenal, and that the *a priori*
knowledge is valid only in relation to phenomena; but I
add that just as phenomenal appearance, it is the
manifestation of that which appears, and with him I call
this the thing in itself. This must therefore express its
nature and character in the world of experience, and
consequently it must be possible to interpret these from
this world, and indeed from the matter, not the mere form,
of experience. Accordingly philosophy is nothing but the
correct and universal understanding of experience itself,
the true exposition of its meaning and content. To this the
metaphysical, *i.e.,* that which is merely clothed in the

phenomenon and veiled in its forms, is that which is related to it as thought to words.

❖

If with this intention we first of all review the interminable series of animals, consider the infinite variety of their forms, as they exhibit themselves always differently modified according to their element and manner of life, and also ponder the inimitable ingenuity of their structure and mechanism, which is carried out with equal perfection in every individual; and finally, if we take into consideration the incredible expenditure of strength, dexterity, prudence, and activity which every animal has ceaselessly to make through its whole life; if, approaching the matter more closely, we contemplate the untiring diligence of wretched little ants, the marvellous and ingenious industry of the bees, or observe how a single burying-beetle (*Necrophorus vespillo*) buries a mole of forty times its own size in two days in order to deposit its eggs in it and ensure nourishment for the future brood (*Gleditsch, Physik. Bot. Œkon. Abhandl.,* iii. 220), at the same time calling to mind how the life of most insects in nothing but ceaseless labour to prepare food and an abode for the future brood which will arise from their eggs, and which then, after they have consumed the food and passed through the chrysalis state, enter upon life merely to begin again from the beginning the same labour; then also how, like this, the life of the birds is for the most part taken up with their distant and laborious migrations, then with the building of their nests and the collecting of food for the brood, which itself has to play the same rôle the following year; and so all work constantly for the future, which afterwards makes bankrupt; then we cannot avoid looking round for the reward of all this skill and trouble, for the end which these animals have before their eyes, which strive so ceaselessly—in short, we are driven to ask. What is the result? What is attained by the animal existence which demands such infinite preparation? And there is nothing to point to but the satisfaction of hunger and the sexual instinct, or in any case a little momentary comfort, as it falls to the lot of each animal individual, now and then in the intervals of its endless need and struggle. If we place the two together, the indescribable ingenuity of the preparations, the enormous abundance of the means, and the insufficiency of what is thereby aimed at and attained, the insight presses itself upon us that life is a business, the proceeds of which are very far from covering the cost of it. This becomes most evident in some animals of a specially simple manner of life. Take, for example, the mole, that unwearied worker. To dig with all its might with its enormous shovel claws is the occupation of its whole life; constant night surrounds it; its embryo eyes only make it avoid the light. It alone is truly an *animal nocturnum*; not cats, owls, and bats, who see by night. But what, now, does it attain by this life, full of trouble and devoid of pleasure? Food and the begetting of its kind; thus only the means of carrying on and beginning anew the same doleful course in new individuals. In such examples it becomes clear that there is no proportion between the cares and troubles of life and the results or gains of it. The consciousness of the world of perception gives a certain appearance of objective worth of existence to the life of those animals which can see, although in their case this consciousness is entirely subjective and limited to the influence of motives upon them. But the *blind* mole, with its perfect organization and ceaseless activity, limited to the alternation of insect larvæ and hunger, makes the disproportion of the means to the end apparent. In this respect the consideration of the animal world left to itself in lands uninhabited by men is also specially instructive. A beautiful picture of this, and of the suffering which nature prepares for herself without the interference of man, is given by Humboldt in his *Ansichten der Natur* (second edition, p. 30 *et seq.*); nor does he neglect to cast a glance (p. 44) at the analogous suffering of the human race, always and everywhere at variance with itself. Yet in the simple and easily surveyed life of the brutes the emptiness and vanity of the struggle of the whole phenomenon is more easily grasped. The variety of the organizations, the ingenuity of the means, whereby each is adapted to its element and its prey contrasts here distinctly with the want of any lasting final aim; instead of which there presents itself only momentary comfort, fleeting pleasure conditioned by wants, much and long suffering, constant strife, *bellum omnium*, each one both a hunter and hunted, pressure, want, need and anxiety, shrieking and howling; and this goes on *in secula seculorum*, or till once again the crust of the planet breaks. Yunghahn relates that he saw in Java a plain far as the eye could reach entirely covered with skeletons, and took it for a battle-field; they were, however, merely the skeletons of

large turtles, five feet long and three feet broad, and the
same height, which comes this way out of the sea in order
to lay their eggs, and are then attacked by wild dogs (*Canis
rutilans*), who with their united strength lay them on their
backs, strip off their lower armour, that is, the small shell
of the stomach, and so devour them alive. But often then
a tiger pounces upon the dogs. Now all this misery repeats
itself thousands and thousands of times, year out, year in.
For this, then, these turtles are born. For whose guilt must
they suffer this torment? Wherefore the whole scene of
horror? To this the only answer is: It is thus that the will
to live objectifies itself.[1] Let one consider it well and

---

1. In the *Siècle*, 10th April 1859, there appears, very beautifully
written, the story of a squirrel that was magically drawn by a
serpent into its very jaws: "Un voyageur qui vient de parcourir
plusieurs provinces de l'ile de Java cite un exemple
remarqueable du pouvoir facinateur des serpents. Le voyageur
dont il est question commençait à gravir Junjind, un des monts
appelés par les Hollandais Pepergebergte. Après avoir pénétré
dans une épaisse forêt, il aperçut sur les branches d'un kijatile
un écureuil de Java à tête blanche, folâtrant avec la grâce et
l'agilité qui distinguent cette charmante espèce de rongeurs. Un
nid sphérique, formé de brins flexible et de mousse, placé dans
les parties les plus élevées de l'arbre, a l'enfourchure de deux
branches, et une cavité dans le tronc, semiblaient les points de
mire de ses jeux. A peine s'en était-il éloigné qu'il y revenait avec
une ardeur extrême. On était dans le mois de Juillet, et
probablement l'écureuil avait en haut ses petits, et dans le bas
le magasin à fruits. Bientôt il fut comme saisi d'effroi, ses
mouvements devinrent désordonnés, on cut dit qu'il cherchait
toujours à mettre un obstacle entre lui et certaines parties de

comprehend it in all its objectifications; and then one will arrive at an understanding of its nature and of the world; but not if one frames general conceptions and builds card houses out of them. The comprehension of the great drama of the objectification of the will to live, and the characterization of its nature, certainly demands somewhat more accurate consideration and greater thoroughness than the

---

l'arbre: puis il se tapit et resta imobile entre deux branches. Le voyageur eut le sentiment d'un danger pour l'innocentre bête, mais il ne pouvait deviner lequel. Il approacha, et un examen atentif lui fit découvrir dans un creux du trone une couleuvre lieu, dardant ses yeux fixes dans la direction de l'écureuil. Notre voyageur trembla pour le pauvre écureuil. La couleuvre était si attentive à sa proie qu'elle ne semblait nullement remarquer la présence d'un homme. Notre voyageur, qui était armé, aurait donc prevenir en aide à l'infortuné rongeur en taunt le serpent. Mais la science l'emporta sur la pitié, et il voulut voir quelle issue aurait le drame. Lc dénoûment fut tragique. L'écureuil ne tarda point à pousser un cri plaintif qui, pour tous ceux qui lc connaissent, dénote le voisinage d'un serpent. Il avança un peu, essaya de reculer, revint encore en avant, tâche de retourner en arrière. Mais s'approcha toujours plus du reptile. La couleuvre, roulée en spirale, la tête au dessus des anneaux, et imobile comme un morceau de bois, ne le quittait pas du regard, L'écureuil, de branche en branche, et descendant toujours plus bas, arriva jusqu'à la partie nue du tronc. Alors le pauvre animal ne tenta même plus de fuir le danger. Attiré par une puissance invincible, et comme poussé par le vertige, il se précipita dans la gueule du serpent, qui s'ouvrit tout à coup démesurement pour le recevoir. Autant la couleuvreavait été inerte jusque là autant elle devint active des qu'elle fut en possession de sa proie. Déroulant ses anneaux et prenant sa course de bas en haut avec

dismissal of the world by attributing to it the title of God, or, with a silliness which only the German fatherland offers and knows how to enjoy, explaining it as the "Idea in its other being," in which for twenty years the simpletons of my time have found their unutterable delight. Certainly, according to pantheism or Spinozism, of which the systems of our century are mere travesties, all that sort of thing reels itself off actually without end, straight on through all eternity. For then the world is a God, *ens perfectissimum, i.e.,* nothing better can be, or be conceived. Thus there is no need of deliverance from it; and consequently there is none. But why the whole tragi-comedy exists cannot in the least be seen; for it has no spectators, and the actors themselves undergo infinite trouble, with little and merely negative pleasure.

Let us now add the consideration of the human race. The matter indeed becomes more complicated, and assumes a certain seriousness of aspect; but the

---

une agilité inconcevable, sa reptation la porta en un clin d'œil au sommet de l'arbre, où elle alla sans doute digérer et dormir."

In this example we see what spirit animates nature, for it reveals itself in it. This story is not only important with regard to fascination, but also as an argument for pessimism. That an animal is surprised and attacked by another is bad; still we can console ourselves for that; but that such a poor innocent squirrel sitting beside its nest with its young is compelled, step by step, reluctantly, battling with itself and lamenting, to approach the wide, open jaws of the serpent and consciously throw itself into them is revolting and atrocious. What monstrous kind of Nature is this to which we belong!

fundamental character remains unaltered. Here also life presents itself by no means as a gift for enjoyment, but as a task, a drudgery to be performed; and in accordance with this we see, in great and small, universal need, ceaseless cares, constant pressure, endless strife, compulsory activity, with extreme exertion of all the powers of body and mind. Many millions, united intonations, strive for the common good, each individual on account of his own; but many thousands fall as a sacrifice for it. Now senseless delusions, now intriguing politics, incite them to wars with each other; then the sweat and the blood of the great multitude must flow, to carry out the ideas of individuals, or to expiate their faults. In peace, industry and trade are active, inventions work miracles, seas are navigated, delicacies are collected from all ends of the world, the waves engulf thousands. All strive, some planning, others acting; the tumult is indescribable. But the ultimate aim of it all, what is it? To sustain ephemeral and tormented individuals through a short span of time in the most fortunate case with endurable want and comparative freedom from pain, which, however, is at once attended with ennui; then the reproduction of this race and its striving. In this evident disproportion between the trouble and the reward, the will to live appears to us from this point of view, if taken objectively, as a fool, or subjectively, as a delusion, seized by which everything living works with the utmost exertion of its strength for something that is of no value. But when we consider it more closely, we shall find here also that it is rather a blind pressure, a tendency entirely without ground or motive.

The law of motivation, as was shown in the First Book, only extends to the particular actions, not to willing *as a whole and in general*. It depends upon this, that if we conceive of the human race and its action *as a whole and universally*, it does not present itself to us, as when we contemplate the particular actions, as a play of puppets who are pulled after the ordinary manner by threads outside them; but from this point of view, as puppets which are set in motion by internal clockwork. For if, as we have done, one compares the ceaseless, serious, and laborious striving of men with what they gain by it, nay, even with what they ever can gain, the disproportion we have pointed out becomes apparent, for one recognizes that that which is to be gained, taken as the motive-power, is entirely insufficient for the explanation of that movement and that ceaseless striving. What, then, is a short postponement of death, a slight easing of misery or deferment of pain, a momentary stilling of desire, compared with such an abundant and certain victory over them all as death? What could such advantages accomplish taken as actual moving causes of a human race, innumerable because constantly renewed, which unceasingly moves, strives, struggles, grieves, writhes and performs the whole tragi-comedy of the history of the world, nay, what says more than all, *perseveres* in such a mock-existence as long as each one possibly can? Clearly this is all inexplicable if we seek the moving causes outside the figures and conceive the human race as striving, in consequence of rational reflection, or something analogous to this (as moving threads), after those good things held out to it, the attainment of which would be a sufficient reward for its ceaseless cares and troubles. The matter being taken thus, everyone would rather have long ago said, "*Le jeu ne vaut pas la chandelle,*" and have gone out. But, on the contrary, everyone guards and defends his life, like a precious pledge entrusted to him under heavy responsibility, under infinite cares and abundant misery, even under which life is tolerable. The wherefore and the why, the reward for this, certainly he does not see; but he has accepted the worth of that pledge without seeing it, upon trust and faith, and does not know what it consists in. Hence I have said that these puppets are not pulled from without, but each bears in itself the clockwork from which its movements result. This is *the will to live,* manifesting itself as an untiring machine, an irrational tendency, which has not its sufficient reason in the external world. It holds the individuals firmly upon the scene, and is the *primum mobile* of their movements; while the external objects, the motives, only determine their direction in the particular case; otherwise the cause would not be at all suitable to the effect. For, as every manifestation of a force of nature has a cause, but the force of nature itself none, so every particular act of will has a motive, but the will in general has none; indeed at bottom these two are one and the same. The will, as that which is metaphysical, is everywhere the boundary-stone of every investigation beyond which it cannot go. From the original and unconditioned nature of the will, which has been proved, it is explicable that man loves beyond everything else an existence full of misery, trouble, pain, and anxiety, and, again, full of ennui, which, if he considered and weighed it purely objectively, he would certainly abhor, and fears above all things the end of it, which is yet for him the one thing certain. Accordingly we often see a miserable figure, deformed and shrunk with age, want and disease, implore our help from the bottom of his heart for the prolongation of an existence, the end of which would necessarily appear altogether desirable if it were an objective judgment that determined here. Thus instead of this it is the blind will, appearing as the tendency to life, the love of life, and the sense of life; it is the same which makes the plants grow. This sense of life may be compared to a rope which is stretched above the puppet-show of the world of men, and on which the puppets hang by invisible threads, while apparently they are supported only by the ground beneath them (the objective value of life). But if the rope becomes weak the puppet sinks; if it breaks the puppet must fall, for the ground beneath it only seemed to support it: *i.e.,* the weakening of that love of life shows itself as hypochondria, spleen, melancholy: its entire exhaustion as the inclination to suicide, which now takes place on the slightest occasion, nay, for a merely imaginary reason for now, as it were, the man seeks a quarrel with himself, in order to shoot himself dead, as many do with others for a like purpose; indeed upon necessity, suicide is resorted to without any special occasion.(Evidence of this will be found in Esquirol, *Des maladies mentales*, 1838.) And as with the persistence in life, so is it also with its action and movement. This is not something freely chosen; but while everyone would really gladly rest, want and ennui are the whips that keep the top spinning. Therefore the whole and every individual bears the stamp of a forced condition; and everyone, in that, inwardly weary, he longs for rest, but yet must press forward, is like his planet, which does not fall into the sun only because a force driving it forward prevents it. Therefore everything is in continual strain and forced movement, and the course of the world goes on, to use an expression of Aristotle's (*De cælo*, ii. 13), "οὐ φύσει, ἀλλὰ βία" (*Motu, non naturali sed violento*). Men are only apparently drawn from in front; really they are pushed from behind; it is not life that tempts them on, but necessity that drives them forward. The law of motivation is, like all causality, merely the form of the phenomenon. We may remark in passing that this is the source of the comical, the burlesque, the grotesque, the ridiculous side of life; for, urged forward against his will, everyone bears himself as best he can, and the straits that thus arise often look comical enough, serious as is the misery which underlies them.

In all these considerations, then, it becomes clear to us that the will to live is not a consequence of the knowledge of life, is in no way a *conclusio ex præmissis*, and in general is nothing secondary. Rather, it is that which is first and unconditioned, the premise of all premises, and just on that account that from which philosophy must *start*, for the will to live does not appear in consequence of the world, but the world in consequence of the will to live.

I scarcely need to draw attention to the fact that the considerations with which we now conclude the Second Book already point forcibly to the serious theme of the

Fourth Book, indeed would pass over into it directly if it were not that my architectonic symmetry makes it necessary that the Third Book, with its fair contents, should come between, as a second consideration of *the world as idea*, the conclusion of which, however, again points in the same direction.